Bronwen Winter Phoenix was born on August 28th, 1985. She has studied journalism, although fictional writing is her true love.

Bronwen finds most of her ideas from dreams, which can happen to be the most vivid, scary, complicated and sometimes delightful things imaginable. She lives in Scotland with her fiancé Tim.

Escaping Dreams

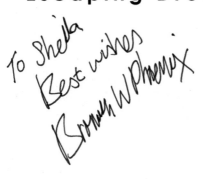

To Sheila
Best wishes

Bronwyn W Phoenix

Bronwen Winter Phoenix

Escaping Dreams

Vanguard Press

A CIP catalogue record for this title is
available from the British Library.

ISBN 978 18438 438 7

Vanguard Press is an imprint of
Pegasus Elliot MacKenzie Publishers Ltd.
www.pegasuspublishers.com

First Published in 2008

Vanguard Press
Sheraton House Castle Park
Cambridge England

Printed & Bound in Great Britain

Dedication

To my family and friends, with love.
Thank you for all your support.
This book is for Tim, who supported me most of all.

Acknowledgements

Acknowledgement to the people who have helped me in their own little ways: this could be friendship, support, advice or just the simplest thing such as reading a part of the book or suggesting a name. Thank you to Aimee Adamson, Blair Kelly, Matts Aerts, Catherine Marois, Jonathan Pow, James Payne, Pascal Zinken, Marina Proud, Andy Slade, Rizia Robertson, Alan Hunter and Kelly Boyd. Also thank you to the late Mary Thompson.

Prologue

Beth

Their noises constant and complete filled every wave there was to fill. She was pushed further by their screams and their deadly force raced behind her, threatening and overpowering. Their thoughts filled her mind and seemed to overload every living part of her until she couldn't work out what was her and what part was them; it was deafening. She could feel it was killing her but she kept going, faster than the speed of light, of thought and of knowledge.

Her terror overtook her soul and she could see them through the corners of both eyes, dark and grasping at her. *They've killed everything.*

She was reaching a point where there would be no return – something she may not survive but something necessary for her soul.

Her senses widened and she pushed even harder into the abyss which slowly drowned out the noise and swept her down into its heart, entering her body and soothing the terror that had filled her.

I thought this day would never come; I'm falling through colours, through light and deep flashes but I'm not scared any more – I've let go.

I think they've stopped following me now, because where I'm going, I may not exist as the same entity.

Maybe they'll stop chasing me now. Maybe they'll let go, like I have learned to let go of them.

Billy

The West Orenian desert was bathed in moonlight; miles from the nearest town, its only long-term residents were the tiny pikan lizards and small insects which roamed the landscape.

Yet something was different tonight, the air had taken on a slightly different quality as if approaching a storm. The desert was silent as if awaiting the messenger's arrival.

Seemingly out of nothing a blue light sparked and then was gone. More appeared in the air just above the sand. The blue rays looked as if they were reaching for something, pulled into broken formations. They emanated a loud crackling noise as if generated by live electricity; they served as a doorway.

A dark form stepped out of the energy field, crouching down in the middle of the lonely desert. The energy field started to crackle even more around them and then to fade, leaving only a trace of blue light before it was gone.

The figure rose to its full height, its skin now pale in the moonlight. It was visible he was male. His head was bald, his eyes shone a bright blue and his lips were full and thick. His muscles looked sculpted; they shone and stood out on his well-developed body.

His mind was cold and empty, his thought process only beginning to awaken from the long journey. Unfocused and clumsy he could not walk yet – only stumble – his anger built up once more for one person; he'd been sent for her, his determination steely and impenetrable. In the sand of the desert, his toes curled feeling his surroundings cautiously.

Looking around, Billy could see there was nothing for miles. Standing fully, he started to walk in the direction of Cial.

Chapter One

Xanther Aerts

The snow had settled down into a light drizzle outside, making everything seem more surreal to him. The street was silent apart from the few cars that drove by, seemingly ignorant of the lone dark figure walking through the dully lit streets, quietly contemplating his mere existence. Despite this, the moon shone down on him like a favoured son although the beauty of this night was shrouded to him. His name was Xanther Aerts.

He was of average height, well-built with dark hair. He was dressed in black. It was the middle of the night and he looked like a normal person out for a walk, in a small Orenian town. But this was no ordinary dark stranger.

He had always been a loner. His life so far had not been long, but the contents had been mournful and sad. Events leading up to the past seven years had caused him to hate the daylight; where people roamed the town, bold and full of confidence, chatting to one another and going about their daily business, carrying bags of shopping and looking in department store windows with curious eyes.

Stepping out into the world only at night, he ordered everything he needed from the internet. He had no family: they died in a plane crash seven years ago, leaving him with the responsibility of a small computer hardware company. He later sold the company to an eager buyer for more than expected.

Xanther had studied computing at university, but it proved too much and it ended after one and a half years of studying and hard work; in small stuffy rooms that had been Magnus University. The depression gripped him like an exquisitely dark velvet glove, something that comforted but shrouded him in darkness, something to hide away from.

The way he'd acted to his friends made sure he lost them, until he had nothing left to lose but life.

Someone had tried to pull him away from the darkness he'd made for himself; she was young and beautiful and deeply in love, sharp the way only your first love can pierce. The pain she felt when he banished her from his life didn't even go so far as to register, apart from deep down in his heart. He told himself it was black, and incapable of love.

Anger towards his parents for dying pushed him towards it, really. But weak as he was, after his failed attempt to end his life with a razor, instead he locked himself in his room for most of the semester until the only option was to fail. Maybe he wasn't that kind of soul. Anyway, that was when he stopped trying. He had hardly ever gone out in the light since.

Turning the corner he came out into Bridge Street. This was not Xanther's usual route. He normally travelled around Moon Walk, where he would usually see Lanai Delores. Delores was a drug dealer. Xanther had seen him around for the past few months but had never sunk low enough to feel the need for his wares. He had seen what it had done to those around him, and it had been a long time since he'd been on lithium.

"Hey, freak! What have you got there?"

Xanther didn't look round. It was a gang of teenagers, one of many that now seemed to control the city. He had learned long ago that the best thing to do was ignore them and keep walking at a steady pace.

"Hey, what's the matter – are you scared?"

Another one joined in. They sniggered.

Xanther continued to walk without looking back.

"That's it…he can't get away with that," said the first one, starting to walk following him down the thin cobbled street.

"Shit, just leave him. He's fucked up; I've seen that guy before…" someone else said.

Xanther never looked back at their immature faces. Ignorant and drugged they stood on the streets most nights drinking from the same bottles they'd later smash and slice with.

Silent, Xanther made his way back up to his dreary flat where he lived alone and had lived that way for a long time. He had never really thought of it as home, instead just somewhere to hide.

When he got there, he unlocked the door, took off his jacket and threw it over the hook. He switched on the light and looked around. It wasn't a pretty sight, but the flat that welcomed him had always been unkempt. No would-be robber had trashed the place, only himself.

Empty beer bottles scattered the floor, the table and the whole room. Chocolate wrappers and other litter lay everywhere. In the kitchen, dirty plates and cutlery lay waiting to be washed while others grew mould. Xanther moved into the bathroom, which was no better. Vomit lay where he had thrown up the night before last. Empty bottles of whiskey and other various kinds of alcohol lay smashed on the carpet. With a sigh, he started to clear up the mess. Something inside him stirred that night, as if realising how unhappy he was deep inside.

Later, he looked up into the mirror and examined himself closely. Thin and bony, pale-faced, bloodshot eyes: he didn't recognise himself. What had he become? He sighed. Perhaps he had given up the will to live. Looking into his dark eyes – the darkest you have ever seen – this is what he saw: a stranger, a loner. He didn't know who he was anymore.

Despite all his internal scars, they didn't show as imperfections on his thin but smooth body. His face knew no bruises, marks, scars. No ugly warts showed as a herald of what lay inside him. No cancer grew like the embodiment of the fear that had taken over his mind.

The past had stayed deep inside him, like an ulcer that would never leave yet was something he drowned out every day with music, movies and television.

Looking at himself, he knew only one thing; he had to wake up. As if it had all been some kind of dream, some strange dark twisted litany of space inside his mind. He needed to somehow get his life back, rescue it before it was too late. The only thing stopping him was his fear; he had lost himself somewhere along the line, his unique agoraphobia becoming a buffer.

He told himself to wake up. Wake up. Wake…up. Wake Up. WAKE UP.

Later, as he lay in bed with sleepy eyes, the light slowly started to filter into the room and he realised he could sleep no longer. In an almost dreamlike state, he experienced one of the only times where things felt real again, the situation he'd put himself in, ridiculous.

Restless, he placed his bare feet on the carpet as he stood up to face the room. His hands made fists, unable to find an outlet for the anxiety that slowly filled him, trickling like the light from the window that now moved over his naked back.

His clothes were mostly old and worn and although the new things he'd purchased seemed like a good idea at the time, it depressed him slightly. They felt out of place in his pathetic wardrobe, and out of place on his body.

Dressing, as he always did in jeans and a t-shirt, dark coloured socks and casual shoes that had never seen daylight, he felt a little calmer. He looks at his hand, which has stopped shaking as he tied his laces, and wondered why he felt so on edge.

He pushed that thought to the back of his mind, because although his conditions seemed to be worsening, it wasn't something he wanted to address.

In an attempt to far remove himself from feeling and from pain, he stooped to the floor and ran his fingers over the worn carpet before reaching for a couple of dirty glasses that'd been placed there days before.

The kitchen was still a mess, and he ran some tap water to wake himself properly before looking around at the dirt. Luckily, the blinds were shut tight so this room was dark.

He sighed, muttering under his breath, "I need to do something about this."

Xanther had never been tidy, but the days seemed to go by hopelessly and with each passing thought his energy levels faded. He thought of it as a downward spiral, forever pulling him in deeper until he was up to his neck in crap.

He smirked, as carefully he picked up a stack of plates and dumped them into the fresh bubbly water; the bubbles originating from a bottle that looked about five years old.

The next hour moved by quickly, each room as unwelcoming as the next. The cold rays of sunlight seemed to judge him and soon his muscles started to ache. It was in the sitting room that eventually, inevitably, he laid the plates back onto the floor and stepped towards the front door.

It stared right back at him, almost taunting him and sweat broke out on his forehead as he stepped forward, closer. It was unyielding, almost menacing although he knew that it would be odd to imagine a door with a conscience. By his side, his hand hesitated to reach forward yet even then he knew, as he always did, that he could go no further. Not now.

A surge of feeling as he punched the wall, filled with self doubt he gave into his weakness. Shaky now, Xanther moved onto the sofa where he'd stay until it all disappeared into a deep but welcome sleep.

A noise, like tapping woke him as he cautiously opened his eyes. He could tell by the light that the day had moved on, and silently he registered his own relief. The room looked different, emptier. Quickly, he remembered he'd tidied up; his own form of displacement therapy. He felt different, as if something was not right and in his confused state, his attention focused towards the door.

Suddenly there was a loud crack as the door was forced open and things seemed to go in slow motion as the figure burst into the room.

Xanther stood up, panic surging through him as Andrew almost fell through the door. He was shouting and gunshots fired loudly as if they were coming from all around the building.

"Get down! They won't stop, Xan, get down!"

Xanther could see the words forming on his best friend's face but felt helpless as Andy stumbled to the floor.

Black figures were soon behind him, all around him in the room and he screamed for them to stop but they were firing at Andy, his body jerking with each shot.

But it wasn't the first time it had happened; the flashbacks warped the room as he saw Andy lying in a pool of blood in the dark concrete floor, the pain flushed through him as he realised the death of his friend.

Young, his eyes filled with hot salty tears as he collapsed onto the floor, unable to care about his own life yet it was too late for that. Guilt surged through him as he thought of all the things he could have done to save Andy and he clutched at the dead body as the figures dressed in black dragged him back to the entrance of his underground.

"No!" he called out above the noise of the faraway gunshots, too weak to fight them off he reached out for Andy once more. They were going to leave him down there, in the dark on the cold floor, why couldn't he stay with him, he wanted to die with him.

He cried out with everything he had, screamed for his grief until everything seemed to fade away into nothing and he collapsed on the sitting room floor.

A loud tap broke the dream, and he woke with a jolt. At first he was confused by his surroundings until he realised he was still lying on the couch.

His emotions felt raw, naked and with surprise he realised his eyes were wet with tears. Turning to the door, he saw no body of Andrew, no sign that the door has been broken yet he had been woken by a noise.

The room was still and quiet as he listened for the source, yet nothing came for a long time. His body felt weak as he pulled himself cautiously out of the sofa.

By instinct, he stepped towards the closed curtains with trepidation and dread, but realised it was the only way to know. He trembled as he reached out and pulled back sharply on the curtain, which ripped from the its fitting and fell to the floor.

Xanther stood frozen as the light hit him, and at first he saw what he had imagined to see; a black figure, come at last to take him back to Andrew.

Instead, two tiny eyes stared into his black ones; a large black crow had rooted itself on his window sill. It squawked, taking him by surprise, its large claws making a loud scraping sound as it shifted position.

"What do you want? Huh?" He whispered as the crow stared through the window. It crooked its head to the left, as if trying to understand the strange looking man with the thick dark stubble.

"Hey, get out of here," he said, louder this time. The crow shifted again before turning and flying away, its dark feathers at first pressed against the window and then gone.

As if suddenly remembering himself, Xanther felt giddy at the light that fell all around him.

Looking down at the single ripped curtain, he swore under his breath before trying to put it back in place. It fell to the ground again.

Out of the window he saw the dingy street, mostly empty apart from a few cars that'd been badly parked. He could hear kids playing in the distance, and he shivered.

Slowly, he backed away from the window, back to his room and the solace of his bed. Later he would remind himself to buy some duct tape.

That night in a different area of town, a man slouched on some steps, hidden from view outside a small, run-down house. He was visibly distraught from the past couple of weeks. He had killed, not for any cause but because he had been forced to. The thing that disturbed him was that he found himself strangely enjoying it. He remembered the feeling well. Now Luke was dead too. He'd been killed by the psycho bitch that never really had a brother. The gang had kept themselves to themselves but when He approached them in their den, offering the chance of power, they listened. But the 'Wolf' had demanded that in exchange for this, she was taken care of too. Neil did not know why he'd chosen their gang as a means of achieving his goal but the Wolf's need was determined and dark. He had found a way into their den, the underground unit that they'd kept hidden from the other gangs. Neil remembered his threatening presence as he sat there; dominating the room he had everyone's attention. His reasons and his need were a secret from the gang and no one seemed to question it. Suddenly, Neil heard footsteps and his thoughts were broken as he turned to the direction they were coming from. It was Timmon, the youngest member of the gang.

"Hey, Neil! The rest of them are on their way," he said.

"Did you bring it?" he said, looking toward the house.

"You bet I did. I don't think we'll have much time though. I think they might have sussed. I've just got a strange feeling…why does he care about her anyway?"

"Yeah, I know what you mean. But she deserves what's coming." Timmon nodded in agreement. The 'she' they were talking about was Beth, Luke's so-called sister. The 'Wolf' had instructed them to start the fire. Now, she would pay for what she had done and news would get out to the Cullens.

Just then, the rest of the gang appeared with Vesrah at the forefront, her short blonde hair glinting under the moonlight. "Let's get this show on the road!" exclaimed Raoul before Timmon produced the gasoline from inside his fleece jacket.

Neil knew this was what they had to do if they wanted to get control of the underground. Following the Wolf had been their only way.

Raoul approached the house as they prepared to light the cloth and said, "He wants us to go ahead with this, not to let her leave."

Neil replied, "You mean lock the door?"

"Yeah, lock the bitch in and watch her burn," Raoul told them. Timmon nodded, kicking the flimsy door hard.

Raoul smiled coldly, ready for the next action that would bring them closer to the Wolf and his promise.

Chapter Two

The Fire

Xanther often ventured out at nights. It was probably the only thing that kept him sane in fact, because his sleep was often filled with haunted nightmares. It was like he was holding some sort of message locked deep within him. It was starting to scare him and he had no idea why.

Andrew, a friend from long ago, still stuck in his mind. They'd grown up together, when the town was a lot calmer than it was now. He had always been able to identify with Andrew, connected with him in many ways. The events of the past drew them even closer before things came to a head, and then the underground seizure happened.

Xanther sometimes heard his voice, when he was alone. A form of his own thinking almost certainly, but comforting anyway – when it was welcome.

They had been fifteen, and renegade youths had only started to form their alliances. A lot was involved, with much to be gained they had the confidence that they needed to fight. They were too young. He'd grown apart from his parents after that, and then to lose them on less than good terms still fell heavy on his heart.

On his nightly walks, he saw all sorts of strange things. Drug dealers roamed the streets, while homeless people slept. Thieves sometimes came and stole from them when they couldn't do anything about it. In the alleys or under the shelter of shop doorways, young couples made love behind the odd dustbin or skip. Middletown was a dangerous place, but not an unusual place. Not normally.

Even though the past trouble was fading, the gangs still existed enough to cause riots, killings and fear. Most of the trouble happened above ground now. The underground had formed a new sort of spirit the past couple of years; a life of its own. Some of the rebels had joined together to create a completely new community and although it was home to the black market, illegal weapon sales and hostiles, it was also open minded and provided safety, if you wanted to join in. Many of the people who lived there sought peace and a home-life they could not have above ground.

Xanther stayed away from people. He saw these things but never took part in them himself. He did not care to help the homeless, or stay and watch the young couples. He had become afraid of this world and the things in it. The underground was certainly off-limits to him. Even though he could feel a hollow ache in his heart, he could not admit to himself he was lonely. At age twenty two, Xanther felt he no longer wanted to carry on living this way.

The gang watched the small house catch fire and spread, slowly at first, then raging with flames so big and bright they could feel the heat on their faces. They stood back a few feet, watching it burn.

A couple of them noticed the brief outline in the shape of a face form in the flames but not distinguished enough to make them think twice. Unexplainable, they cast glances at each other, smiling stupid smiles. It could almost be said that they had no minds, like something was happening somewhere, but they were too preoccupied with gang life to notice the mental and physical changes that slowly manifested within themselves. And Neil would tell them that they knew this task had to be done. No one could argue with that. The form flashed slightly in the heat of the fire, and then was gone.

"Man, this is risky," said Timmon, "If we don't want to get caught we should get the hell out of here."

"Agreed," said Neil, already starting to leave as a light switched on in the street. Vesrah, dressed completely in black, swiftly dragged Neil to the side as they ran off into the night, followed by Raoul, disappointed and last to leave as the screams echoed down the street.

He recalled the Wolf's voice, deep and harsh, warning him not to leave the fire until it was time.

"Fuck that," he whispered.

Sitting in front of a late night horror movie, Xanther grew restless. The bottle of vodka he had bought the night before was now empty, and he had no other alcohol left in the house. Having nothing else to preoccupy his – still half sober – mind with, his thoughts returned once more to the tragedy of his life. He sat up. He knew it was silly and unhealthy to wallow in self-pity and because he had not yet reached the suicidal stage, he decided the only thing to do was go out again. He didn't want to but… he heard Andrew's voice, as he sometimes did when he was alone.

So, once more, Xanther put on his long black coat and went out to the streets of Middletown just like every other night, although unknown to him this was not an ordinary night. Something he sensed made him feel uneasy but it lay ignored, deep down in his mind.

He felt the wind, icy cold against his face as soon as he opened the door. Shivering, he began to make his way down the

28

deserted street and once again into the darkness of the night. Something in him stirred, and walking along Bridge Street, he decided to take a different route. He felt adventurous tonight and didn't want to go home so soon. He decided to take a left turn instead and go along Maple Street. Taking a quick sideways glance, he was glad to see that no one was around. This street was in the poorer and more dangerous area of Middletown and he most probably had a good chance of getting mugged. Not that he could care much.

He looked at his watch and saw that it was now 3:16 am. He had been contemplating why he'd left the flat for longer than he cared to register now. He was finding the night breeze refreshing and so kept going, as if fuelled by an energy to find himself, needing to expel it in some way.

From there he turned into Jacob Terrace. Another bad but not-so-bad area of town, shabby and run-down. Not many occupied this street.

At first everything looked normal but then he stopped. Members of one of the gangs were running from something as he turned the corner at the end of the street. He was glad they never saw him.

Middletown was a dying town, plagued by gangs who craved power and something to do. The feuds and fighting only led to more violence and hatred. The government eventually drove a lot of them underground, which only seemed to make things worse because under the streets of Middletown, lay what could be seen as a completely new community. The old waterways had been unused for decades, and the growing community of the underground was a great topic of debate, despair and tragic hope for those who fuelled the rebellion.

He smelled smoke. Looking to the end of the street he saw that one of the houses had been set alight.

He felt his heartbeat increase and he started jogging towards the house at the end of the terrace. It was not every day that he witnessed a fire and something pulled him towards the flames. He could see the fire burning brightly now and the noise was loud, like he remembered hearing when he was a child at one of the bonfires his father had taken him to. Like a crackling sound. Then, to his surprise, a louder noise rose through all the crackling. It was a scream: a girl's scream to be precise.

Xanther looked up at one of the windows and saw a girl looking down at him. "Help me! Please call for help!"

Looking around, Xanther saw the whole street was deserted. He was not surprised.

Going to run away? The thought echoed through his head.

"Yes," he whispered to himself.

Looking back at the girl who was almost hysterical now, he made up his mind to run. After all he had had no idea that this house was occupied. He had thought this area of town had been deserted. Most houses on the street were empty and up for rent.

"Please help…" the girl said. Then she disappeared from the window.

Xanther didn't know what to do. He wanted to run. He was scared. But then she would die. He ran to the house.

The closer he got to the fire, the more he could feel the heat radiating from it. His heart was racing in his chest. He had never felt this alive – this real – for years. The door was slightly indented. Touching the handle almost burned his skin but he managed to force it open, pushing on it with the sleeve of his jacket.

Strangely he had never imagined himself doing such a thing as he registered the ridiculousness of the situation.

The inside of the house was filled with bright orange flames. He could hear the young girl screaming at the top of her voice again. He searched the room, looking for a staircase.

He saw one across the hall, hesitated and ran towards it, coughing from the lethal fumes. It was blocked by the loud, crackling fire.

Looking around he could see the wallpaper peeling off the walls, all black and burnt. It reminded him of when he was fifteen, and just like a kid out of his depth again. Then he heard a loud noise from the ceiling as a large beam fell to the floor. The house was quite literally falling apart all around him. He thought about running away again, being a coward, but knew it was too late now. He took a deep breath and ran at the stairs as fast as he could. The heat was almost unbearable, but when he came out at the other side, he saw he was not burned at all.

"Help!" cried the woman. He saw she was standing looking out the window, not knowing he was behind her.

"Hey! I'm here!" He shouted through the sound of the flames and she turned towards him quickly. She gasped. Xanther noticed for the first time how striking she was, surrounded by the orange light of the flames. She ran towards him screaming.

"Oh my God, thank you!" She looked up at him. "I thought you'd gone. Thought I was going to die..." She sobbed and put her arms around him. At first he stepped back, scared, but then he hugged her back.

"We've got to get out of here, now!" he shouted.

"You don't understand. They'll chase me wherever I go and they'll stop at nothing! Why don't you just leave me here to burn and protect yourself! They'll take me. Let them take me!" But her crying had turned to fits of coughing. He lifted her up and ran back towards the stairs. To his dismay, they were now nearly completely blocked by the rising flames. It took him all the courage he had left to run at it. He managed to run right through the fire, screaming and holding the woman in his arms. She was so light and fragile, as if he might break her. She was still screaming so loudly it hurt his ears, and what she was saying didn't make any sense to him. The whole house was ablaze by now and Xanther could hear fire engines approaching. The next time he looked down at her, she was unconscious. He had to get out or soon he would be too. He was starting to feel light-headed. Before him a shadowy figure seemed to rush out of the flames and through towards the back of the house. A hallucination, he nevertheless decided to follow, desperate to find a way out of the burning frenzy that now surrounded him and the girl. The kitchen was less affected by the fire, and he was in there alone. The door opened.

Somehow, he found himself standing outside on the grass a couple of minutes later.

He watched stupidly as the fire trucks came round the bend. They were soon accompanied by an ambulance. The firemen rushed to the flames as the paramedics came and took the girl out of his arms. As soon as they had done so, he fainted and darkness entered his mind.

In and out of consciousness, he drifted. Focusing, he realised he was looking up at a white ceiling. He had a funny taste in his mouth. Then it all came back to him. He sat up. A young nurse was staring at him.

"I said, can you tell me your name?"

"Huh?"

"Your name?" She looked at him slightly bemused.

"Xanther," he managed to stutter.

"You're in hospital, Xanther. You're all right now. You just fainted."

"I know…"

"That was a very heroic thing you did back there, you know?"

"Pardon?"

"Saving that girl, I mean. Could have gotten you killed."

"Oh," he said, suddenly remembering the girl's face among all the flames and the heat, "Is she all right?"

"Yes, she should be. She just got a mild case of smoke inhalation. Do you feel okay?"

"Yeah, I'm fine now. Can I see her, please?" he asked the nurse, desperate to get out of the bed.

"Sure, in a couple of minutes. Do you know her?"

"Nope, sorry."

"I'm just checking on her now. Back soon." And she left him in the room by himself. Looking around he could see posters and empty beds and other equipment. There was nothing unusual. The hospital was eerily empty, like a lot of the town these days. Perhaps it was the particular ward but there was something run-down, uneasy, about it. She came back in.

"The girl's completely exhausted, I'm afraid. She's in Ward 10, just down the hall. But I think you should rest here for now. Your body's probably still in shock. Spend the night, just to be safe. Do you have any relatives we could contact?"

"Ermmm... no, actually. I'd rather just go home and rest there, if that's all right with you. I feel fine, really."

The nurse sighed, "Well, I'm afraid I can't let you do that, Xanther. The authorities will arrive soon for questioning. It's just standard procedure. Oh, and your jacket's at the desk down there, just so you know."

He waited until she left, sighed and stood up slowly to get his jacket. He was just about to go when he changed his mind and decided to see the girl one last time. Her ward was just across the room and it wouldn't hurt. She was asleep anyway, he reasoned. She wouldn't know any different.

Her room was empty and dull. She was just lying there, hands by her sides, fast asleep. She was so thin. Again he was taken aback by her beauty. She was about his age, her long dark brown hair spread out across her pillow. He walked over to her and sat down on the chair beside her bed. He realised he couldn't take his eyes off her. Sitting there, admiring her pretty face, he wished he could get to know her a little better. But of course, he knew he was dreaming. A lonely freak like him could never have someone like her. She was so beautiful, so delicate, and so

33

mysterious even just lying there, totally defenceless. He wondered what her life was like, and who she really was. Even lying there in a hospital bed, looking as pale as she did, he still felt warmth for her.

What was she doing there, of all places, alone in that barn of a house? Why wasn't there someone there to protect her?

He remembered some of the things she had been shouting while he had rescued her, and still couldn't make sense of any of it. All he knew was that she was in some kind of trouble that she wanted to escape from but couldn't. He couldn't understand how deeply she was involved, or how easily he could get pulled in. Even as he was thinking these things, he fell asleep at her side.

Chapter Three

Beth's Dream

I had another dream. We were on a modern bridge, travelling over the water. There were many cars and it was a strange bridge really. It had two levels to it; we were on the lower one. I was with my beloved, and Emma was driving. It was a clear day, bright and calm.

I felt happy to be with my beloved, Tristan; we sat together but I felt something was wrong. I felt nervous; I don't really like cars at the best of times. He was looking at me, and I was looking at him and his hands felt so warm holding mine. I would give anything to experience that again. He had the warmest smile, his hair soft yet untamed. Thinking about him now is too painful.

Anyway, I started to fidget. We were approaching the middle of the bridge, and I heard the sound of a large helicopter. It was behind us, making its way unsteadily upwards, it had come from underneath. I knew it was here for us.

I tried to stay calm and tightly held onto his arms as he looked back at the helicopter. I willed it to leave us alone, finally for them to leave us alone. I used my mind gift. As the helicopter came closer it was still rising. Emma was silent, but she started to drive faster; a look of panic had come over her face too.

I think I did it. I think I killed them. The helicopter hit the floor of the upper level, crushing the top and causing it to come crashing down. Emma managed to get us out the way of the impact but we were thrown off the bridge by the force of the fall. I screamed as we flew through the air, to land in the sea below. I had hold of the door and as soon as we crashed down and started to sink, we all managed to get out of the car. It was official; we were on the run again.

The next thing I remember was that there were 6 of us, two others that I used to know well and Sylvia, my younger sister. We were in the old glen, somewhere that used to be calm for us, peaceful. I cannot tell you for how long I have wished to be back there.

But now it was different. We were being hunted, chased by people. What had we done to hurt them? We were running. Our car had run out of petrol and two men were chasing us. Soon, a woman followed; they had knives.

In front of us there was an old house. We got inside, tried to board up the doors. We were shouting to each other, trying to find things to barricade the openings. We had entered through a broken window, the door still intact. There were many windows, and for now I motioned silence. We had managed to outrun the intruders. Hopefully, if we just hid in the shadows of this house, we would be fine.

Tristan and I hid together, and I do not know how long it was we stayed there but I slept. When I awoke, I heard the others. Tristan was still at my side, looking at me.

"Look at this place," I whispered to him. The house was bare, hardly anything of worth held in it. What was there was old and dirty, dusty or covered with sheets. The room they were in held some kind of machinery, lots of metal. It smelled rusty.

The house was dark now. There were no lights. I slowly stood up, and followed the voices of the others into the main room where we had entered. The windows were sealed. They had used mud, mixed with leaves and stone. A couple were boarded up. I shivered, as it was cold.

I cannot remember how long I was out there, watching the sun go down over the endless rows of fields and countryside. It was quite a long time. The sun was bloody; a large red smear glowed down on us from the orange-red sky. As I sat in silence, I realised this may be the last sunset I was to see.

I was wrapped in my green woollen shawl, hugging myself tight as I sat on the top of a small hill near the cabin. The wind rattled through a nearby tree, making me shiver. The cold had settled into my bones by now, and I thought of the warm fire, beckoning me inside. Our small cabin was still visible in the distance.

I felt small, sitting there alone. Everything was beautiful and even though I had been wishing for this to finally come to an end after all this time, I wanted to be on this earth forever. It was a perfect night.

I slowly stood up, my legs feeling slightly numb, and I began to make my way back to our temporary house. I could make out the vague silhouette of one of my sisters, waiting for me on the porch. We all knew our time together now was short, and I think we were all slightly on edge with the waiting.

Not long after, I had made my way safely back to the cabin. The door was open for now, and I let myself in.

Sylvia was inside, her gaze fixed on the place the sun had been. She looked up as I entered the room.

"Did you lock the door?" she asked.

"Yes. Don't worry so much," I whispered as I passed her. Emma was the oldest, Sylvia the youngest. I was the middle child.

We had been living here in obscurity, hidden away for five months now, and we knew that as the nights drew in quicker and the days grew shorter, our chances of making it through to next year were starting to dim. It seemed unreal, that we were here and surviving. We all sensed our time was indeed very, very close. When I looked into Sylvia's eyes, I didn't like the abyss of fear that stared back at me. Perhaps she had the most powerful gift of us all, which frightened me somewhat. She had grown very sluggish the past few weeks, barely going outdoors.

"The colours tonight are very beautiful," said Emma, who had entered from the kitchen. "The red is one of the most vivid I've seen in a long time." I nodded, and managed a small smile. She carried a bowl filled with a similar colour of dye.

"It inspired me," she continued. "Hopefully this will strengthen our bond together. This is similar to henna, I want to paint our hands."

I watched as she carried out this delicate task on herself first. She used a brush with a tiny point, and began to paint a small dark red circle filled with detail on the back of her left hand. Emma, always the artistic one, believed in our bond and that with our bond, we could achieve anything. Maybe she believed that whatever tiny thread this may sew, it could keep us together and help us to win the eventual battle.

They were coming for us; there was no doubt about that. We had managed to hide ourselves away in a tiny cabin a long way from anything we knew, but perhaps that did not matter and wherever we were, they would have come for us anyway.

Emma's design looked very symbolic, but its meaning eluded me. I trusted her to do whatever she thought was right, and Sylvia volunteered herself next. She received a vine design, which covered most of the left side of her hand in thin dark lines.

"Your turn, Beth," Emma told me.

As I rested my hand on the table, I glanced at the dresses. They were sort of ceremonial. We would wear them when we felt the time had come. We weren't altogether powerless; we would attack like cornered cats when the time came. But compared to the Chaka, we were weak.

38

"Your hand is shaking," Emma said soothingly. I looked into her eyes and could sense what she was thinking. Sylvia's fear was now our own too. On my hand, she painted a small and delicate nymph. She spent the longest on my design; the cool feel of the brush relaxed me. I smiled painfully as she started to take the bowl and brush away.

We hadn't had television since we moved here, and we had no idea what was going on in the world. Our little cabin was all we had. So quiet in our world, the wildlife crowded around us and we grew accustomed to that being the only continuous sound. I followed Emma to the kitchen.

"Emma…" Her back was facing me as she was leaning over the sink. Her boots tapped quietly on the floor.

"Don't let it be tonight…" she told me. Her voice wavered on the last word.

"I know. I know. I hope they don't come," I replied. She turned to face me and her eyes told me she knew they would. I tried to ignore the bond we'd had since we were children, I tried not to read her thoughts and instead her fear caught hold of me. I stepped forward, held her.

"It's going to be all right," I whispered in her ear. She whimpered slightly before gathering her breath.

"Maybe we should get some sleep. I feel really tired," I said. She nodded and without saying another word she left the room.

I lit a candle that night. Its yellow flame started to dance as I stared into it, cupping my hands around it. The heavy curtains in my room were shut tight and I hoped did not show much light to the outside world. I took it over to my bedside and laid it on the small wooden table.

It was cold in my small room; I crawled under the covers of my bed fully clothed. I fixed my eyes on the candle, my face close so I could feel a small amount of the heat.

I stared until the flame melted into my vision and I began to feel like I was moving away; out of my surroundings. I began to see shapes, tiny little moving shapes and I realised I could hear screaming, very slight and far away in my head. They were women's laughing screams, and a man's terror, twisted and deep. The figures were getting more visible, and in the middle of my focus I saw a face start to melt in to the picture. A face so terrible and frightening it has burned my memory and I will never forget it. So far, this is the only image I have of what killed my sisters.

It was a mistake. I used to use the same gift all the time when I was younger, but I stopped when I heard my name being called.

I went to sleep shaking with tears in my eyes, the wind howling outside and the candle burnt out and lying overturned on the floor.

We were in the fields out back in the dark. It was cold and I was wearing the red and white dress. I could hear screams, and terror pulsed through my body. Something brushed beside my leg and I cried out.

Sylvia. Sylvia was screaming but I didn't know which direction the sound was coming from. I put my hands up to my ears, and the noise stopped, followed by Emma's "Shhhh!"

"Emma…?" I ask in a small voice. I tried to make my way forward but the grass was tall and I almost stumbled.

"Beth, come closer!"

I could make out two huddled shapes by now, and I slowly walked towards them.

"Oh God, oh God, oh God," whispered Sylvia. They were out there. We could all feel it. I didn't really think being quiet would save us. Emma's hand reached out for mine, gripping me tight and pulling me forward.

"We need to get help. We need to run and find help," I whispered. I told them to stay where they were and I ran. My dress dragged and ripped in the bushes and long grass, I could feel something over us like a dead weight, a dark cloud. The stars shone brightly in the sky as I looked up, but the moon was nowhere in sight. When I reached the top of the hill I knew there was a small stone cottage, I could sense its lights and I made this my goal. I shouldn't have left my sisters, I shouldn't have. Everything was quiet except from my pounding heart and my gasping breath.

I stumbled, almost tripping over the long material of my dress. I had reached the hill now and I pulled myself up straight, wiping the dirt from my hands. It was in darkness. I could see no cottage, only black ahead of me. It was like the fields went on forever and no lights showed in the distance.

It was then I heard the scream. It went on for about three seconds before it was abruptly cut off. I couldn't make out the voice, and shaking, I slowly turned around. I was crying, my entire body shaking and I'd never been so scared. They were here for us.

It felt like forever, half-running unsteadily down the hill. I felt like I was in a trance. There were no more noises. My head felt cloudy and dizzy. My heartbeat had slowed back to normal and everything seemed more real when I stood at the bottom of the hill. I had no idea how much time had passed and I listened to the silence, confused. My pace sped up as I searched the long grass. I could see nothing in front of me, nothing to either side but more grass. It covered the whole field and I couldn't make out figures anywhere.

It was then my foot hit something. Dread sunk into me and I slowly leaned down to touch the first blood drenched body.

"No… oh no…" I was defeated. The tears streamed down my face. Why did they have to do this to us! I got up, soaked in blood myself. I knew I was next but I didn't care.

"Emma!" I cried. I rushed around, aimlessly looking until I found the body of my other dead sister. Holding her in my arms, I stopped crying. They were coming for me now, and whatever happened, I hated them. I was going to fight, and I hoped that before I died, I caused some damage.

I woke up, my body covered in sweat and shaking like a leaf. It was the same darkness as in my dream, and for a few seconds I felt the same fear and anguish, the same overpowering hate. Then it faded and I looked around, confused. I was in my room; it was the still of night.

My heart was beating fast as I slowly got up. Emma was asleep on the couch, holding a penknife. She was wearing the same dress.

Sylvia was too young when it happened, to have remembered what had killed our parents. My Tristan, now perhaps dead too; my loss echoed deep in my mind.

I hurried outside. It was dark still and I clutched my bag in my hands. They were coming, I could feel it. I found myself running and then walking, a sense of terror deep inside my heart. I felt it now: there was no going back. I needed to get to the next village. The sun was slowly starting to come up and with the light of the day I saw the houses in the distance. I knew I shouldn't be on my own, I felt like I was leaving something terrible behind at the same time and all I felt was that I wanted to run. I had a hope but also a terror of perhaps leading these horrible creatures away from my sisters. I felt so confused, my mind racing. I couldn't be left alone, not for one minute. I needed the city and the noise. I needed to hide from them. The pink nymph was on my hand. She stared up at me. The joints in my hips were aching slightly; I must have been walking for almost five hours. As I approached the first house, I felt a darkness near me. I shivered and decided to walk on the larger path; they were separated by a hill. The outer one was beside a large drop and I could feel a presence there. I walked faster, and sensed I was close to people. I stopped to ask an elderly woman where the bus stop was. She told me it was in the square. I passed the church and saw a policeman and three villagers talking outside. They mentioned praying our family name. My sisters were dead. I knew they would be coming for me now and I would not have time to grieve. I'd found the square; I needed to get to a city fast. I clutched my Brothern amulet to my chest like some sort of protective talisman, and prayed to be set free.

It occurred to me I might be the only one of my race left and as I slowly fell asleep on the bus, my body exhausted, I allowed myself to rest; for now.

My memories… She gasped and woke with a start, before realising once more that none of this was real any more. She opened an eye to see him lying beside her in the dark room. But even though her memories haunted her sleep, fear gave way to exhaustion and she was plunged back into unconsciousness as quickly as she'd awoken. Far away, perhaps only in her mind, distant chimes played softly. Sleeping beauty lay still.

Chapter Four

The Hospital

For a moment, Xanther did not know where he was. He woke up with his head at someone else's bedside. His neck hurt. With shock, he realised it was daytime. The sun was out and he realised he must have slept at the hospital all night. With increasing dread, he noticed he was staring down at the girl he had rescued the night before. He knew he had no right, sitting at a complete stranger's bedside all night, especially when he didn't even know her name. And what if she had woken up to see him sleeping there?

He quickly stood up, threw on his jacket – he must have taken it off – and quickly stumbled towards the door.

"Wait, don't go…" he heard the girl say. He turned around. He had no idea she'd been awake. "I don't even know your name. You rescued me last night, didn't you?"

His face turned a whiter shade of pale. "Well, yes."

She smiled at him. She was making him feel uncomfortable, the way her beauty pierced through his heart. "Thank you for saving my life. I thought you ran away before…I thought I was going to die." Her voice broke slightly and she looked down at her hands. "It was very sweet of you to visit me.

Are you all right? You didn't have to stay here all night did you?"

He smiled. "No, of course not. I was worried about you so I just dropped by to see that you were all right. I was just passing the hospital and I thought...." He was babbling.

"Oh. Well thank you. What's your name?"

"Xanther Aerts," he stammered.

"I'm Beth Elretha."

After an awkward silence, he opened his mouth to mutter something about leaving soon or perhaps being late for something, when she spoke.

"Possessions... what are they to me? I loved that house but who was I kidding..." He looked at her, perturbed by her words.

"Do you know why they did it?" he asked. She looked at him with a sad smile.

"No, but starting again is nothing new to me," she replied.

"I wish I had your courage," he sighed, "I'd have tried that years ago." Her hand reached out and touched his, and she looked into his eyes. He thought of a thousand souls, all reaching through to him, searching, gentle, although surely there was only one he was in the presence of right now.

"So, how are you?" she asked him, a trace of a smile forming on her lips.

"Better now," he replied. She answered this with a slightly confused look, before they were interrupted.

"Hello again, Xanther. Enjoy your rest? I thought about waking you, but you really looked like you needed the sleep. Sorry. You didn't get a sore neck, did you?" The nurse asked politely.

Xanther looked at Beth, then back to the nurse again. "Erm... no," he muttered.

"Wow..." Beth uttered. "You slept here all night, didn't you?" She smiled sweetly. There was something about him, she noticed.

"I'm sorry. I kind of… fell asleep," he looked embarrassed.

"Just completely gone, you were. Are you feeling better today, Miss?"

"Yes, much, thank you."

They went through the usual rigmarole of questions and tests, and after a tedious forty-five minutes they were finally given permission to leave. It all seemed sort of distant to Xanther, like echoes, they blurred. He realised this was probably because he hadn't really slept much, and felt rather spaced out.

"Well, I don't know what happened to the police," the nurse continued, "I thought they'd probably ask you a few quick questions about what happened last night."

"Oh, I'll go down there and tell them all I know. I don't know what started the fire, really," Beth said to her. The nurse nodded and left the room.

Beth turned to Xanther, "I have a feeling we should get out of here." He looked at her, then at the windows which showed the bright sun. It'd been a long time since he'd ventured out during the day, but all of a sudden, it didn't seem like a bad idea.

"Prison break?" he replied.

They started to walk out together, although his legs felt slightly detached from his body and kind of jelly-ish. She grasped his hand and he noticed she looked kind of weak, just like he felt. There was a strange feeling in the air. The atmosphere of the hospital wasn't quite right. Maybe it was the shabby walls, the emptiness of the many beds, or the quietness of the ward. Overhead lights flickered on Ward 9, which made Beth shudder. *Like something from Frankenstein, they're sewing the dead bits together in there.*

A face in the flickering became visible in the window. Her gaze fixed on it as they passed. The feeling of foreboding built up deep inside.

A sense of something wrong seemed to be in the air as they passed Ward 9. Xanther felt it. His legs felt more and more like jelly, and then it seemed to happen in slow motion. It started like a build-up of energy behind them, a darkness which didn't exactly feel like solid matter but like it was only just materialising from somewhere else. He didn't dare turn around to see, because this thing, this feeling terrified him and there was no time then to make any sense of this feeling. Beth seemed to stiffen. She turned to him, her eyes caught his, held them and she said one word: "Run."

They ended up in a café. It was old and kind of shabby, but it was open and proved a formidable and welcome distraction. It was one of those places where you could have a snack at any time of the day. It was popular. Xanther had never been around so many people at once for a long time. At first it had made him slightly nervous, but he soon was able to relax with Beth at his side. They chose a table near the windows, a shaded little alcove. Beth confided in him that this was her favourite spot, mainly because you could see everyone come and go but they could not spot you so easily. She also told him she worked as a waitress in a small restaurant in town on Wednesdays, Thursdays and Sundays, in the evenings. She confided in him that she didn't mind having such a small job as so much of her life had been preoccupied with other things.

Xanther learned a lot about her in those fifteen minutes and the more he learned, the more he liked about her.

She looked at him more closely now. He seemed very different to anyone she'd been around in a long time. His presence made her feel at ease, like someone else used to make her feel. She liked his face, the way he held her gaze and the way he looked at things like he was seeing everything for the first time. What she found strange though, were his eyes. They were a beautiful, dark colour, almost black and she'd never seen anything like them before. Apart from that, his face was not that distinctive. It had a handsome, honest quality like his mere

47

innocence was a physical thing. His skin was so pale and she wondered if he had recovered from a recent illness.

She could also tell he was quiet, but whether it was down to inexperience or life, she wasn't sure. When they had left the hospital he had seemed really quite nervous. He asked her questions about herself, and she answered as best she could. Knowing that he would just keep babbling all day if she didn't stop him, she decided to move on to another subject entirely.

"So, how old are you, Xanther?"

"Twenty-two," he answered.

"I'm twenty-three." She sighed. She looked out the window, at the people walking by. One man, probably on his way to work, dropped his briefcase. Beth smiled, but then it seemed like a dark cloud came over her face, "What will I do? I don't want to see the house, but I'll need to see what's left with my own eyes."

Xanther hesitated. She seemed to be keeping something hidden from him but he could tell she had dealt with a lot of pain recently.

He said, "I suppose I've got nothing else to do, I can help you look." He knew it would need more than just help, but he didn't know what else to say. He was enjoying this time with her, despite the strange circumstances.

She seemed not to notice. Finishing her coffee, she said "It's not far from here. Let's go." So they went. Xanther started to feel awkward, and tried to improve her mood a little.

"So, do you live by yourself?"

"Yes."

"Same here, although I don't really have much choice."

They walked on in silence for a while. Beth looked strangely calm, serene, despite what had happened last night. Nevertheless, she looked fragile and her clothes looked slightly charred, making the moment even more surreal. She turned to him.

48

"You can leave if you want, you know," she told him, "I'm more than adequately capable of coping with this myself. I'll find a way."

"I know. But I don't want to." He looked so serious, it made her smile. She was grateful for that.

"Good, I don't want you to leave me," she replied. Her eyes brightened for a second, and then it was gone.

"I don't like what's happening to this place," he said.

"Where do you work?"

"I don't."

"Really?"

"Really."

"Can you afford that? I mean, how do you live?"

"My parents left me a lot of money when they died, and I've been going through a rough patch."

"I know what that's like," she smiled sadly.

"Why are you living here?"

"It's my home, basically. I've never felt the need to move anywhere else."

"If I had the money, I know that I'd move away from here straight away." She examined him.

"Why would you be so eager to move away from here?"

"I'm not really from around here. I'm no stranger to moving."

"What about friends?"

"Real ones? None really, nor family for that matter. The gangs set fire to my house." Her voice broke and she looked away from him. It pained him to see her so broken. He could imagine her without these troubles.

"Gangs? Of course. I saw them running away before I noticed you. Why did they target you? What did you do to them?"

Middletown was dominated by gangs. When they weren't underground, they roamed the streets looking for trouble every night. The whole town was turning violent.

"I'm not sure, but I've got a very bad feeling about it.

Chapter Five

Aime

The isolated Aime building was dark from the outside, unknown to passers-by apart from a certain sense of electricity in the air almost undetectable to most senses.

It was built on private land, isolated by trees and a long country path leading up to the estate.

Deep inside the core of the building, the atmosphere was thick with tension; the air sterile inside rooms devoid of colour.

Steifler was at the forefront, the 'main man' of the operation. He wore the standard white coat, anti-static gloves and the ID of one P.D. Manson. His thick glasses shielded his eyes and partially his pale face, his light-mousy hair was cut short.

Hours of hard work had been spent to create the specifications barely memorable to him now; as if he had been deep in concentration. It seemed like a dream, but somehow he had completed the work and they were ready to test the new dimensions.

When they had stormed the building two weeks ago under the 'Wolf' orders, Steifler knew beforehand that the crew involved were doing something less than stable, experimenting with sub-force lasers. But he had no idea to what extent they had built them until he saw this baby.

It stood before him now, humming softly, its metallic glow bright under the white lights overhead.

He and his colleagues had been paid a ridiculous amount of money for this operation, and now he knew exactly why. In Cial they had been working on generators and sub-reactors and only had a basic knowledge of laser-bolt technology. Now, they worked day and night in order to structure the components and create what the 'Wolf' needed.

They had only ever communicated with the Wolf's angry snarl by phone. Originally approached by a gang of thugs, they had been given a cheque and forced to travel from their hometown in Cial.

The specifications the 'Wolf' had given him could in theory open up something completely unknown to him. As far as he was aware the instructions he'd been given were crazy – there was no way of knowing what the 'rip' they created would lead to.

The machine's hum seemed to increase and he knew it was almost time for the first test. The 'Wolf' was now on his way.

Steifler joined the developers, his team, now assembled behind the flex screen, ready to initiate the start-up sequence.

Steifler turned to one of his team-mates, Angler, and said, "Are we ready?"

Angler nodded, a thumbs-up visible through his anti-static gloves. The team started up the laser procedure, making the lights momentarily flicker.

The fans swooped into life, the lights counting down to launch time. The room grew noticeably warmer as they waited in suspense.

Suddenly everything seemed to slow down, the lights dimmed and the fans stopped. For a couple of seconds it seemed to malfunction before a bright light entered the room, temporarily blinding most of the team. The laser was making a terrible shrieking noise, shaking as if it was about to explode. The room seemed unsteady, as if the very fabric of reality was bending and twisting, shaping to form something new. The air almost looked like it was melting around them. Steifler felt himself floating, falling deep into an unconsciousness filled with fear and fury. One thought entered his mind, *what have we done.*

When he awoke, the light had focused on one part of the room; a large gaping hole bright with colour.

That's not all; something was coming from inside the huge tear in the space around them. A large dark beast charged forward, not quite there yet, solid and threatening. Dazed, Steifler lay frozen on the floor, watching as it shook one of the men between its teeth. Crawling away, he noticed with horror that it was Angler, his blood seeping onto the once sterile white floor. The tear had given birth to a second beast by the time Steifler managed to crawl to the door, his secure-card slotting into the lock with great difficulty. The door opened and Steifler screamed at the rush of hot air as the beasts burst through into the building and out into the night air only moments later.

In the heart of Middletown, Sam Cullen called a meeting. Neil had gone too far the other night. But it wasn't just that he was worried about. He was worried for the gang too; all had gone quiet in their area and they had made many enemies.

Looking around, Sam could see that five of them were present. He had a headache. Sighing, he got up and walked to the middle of the room. "Okay, since most of us are here, I think I'd better inform you of our plan," he said. There was mutterings from all around the shaded room. Sam went on, "It seems that Luke was right. About Neil, I mean." The five of them all looked up at Sam with the same horror. Sam was the oldest of the five brothers and everyone treated him with respect.

Vincent interrupted him, running into the room with a look of panic on his face, his breathing heavy and scared.

"Vince… what's wrong?" Sam asked, as the others turned to face his younger brother.

"I saw them. They were dragging something into the warehouse, God knows what," Vincent replied.

"Okay, calm down," Sam told him, "Take a seat and tell us."

"I don't know what this thing was, but it was massive and it was breathing – no rasping – and some others saw it too. It wasn't under control. At one point Raoul had to shoot it."

Sam sighed, "What the fuck is going on down there…first Beth and now this."

They were all very worried about Beth, but had heard from a source that she was all right.

"Yeah, that's right. They're more dangerous and unpredictable than we thought. We have to do something about it because it's not right….who knows what they've got planned next?" Daire spoke up. He'd been watching the gang for a while. He didn't trust them one bit.

"Was Luke right about… you know… the other thing?" asked Kordian. Vince gave his brother a hard look of warning.

Sam looked down at his hands. "I don't know. There are sources, yes… sources who say that they have heard strange noises at night. Sources that say they have found strange implements with blood on them that have been discarded in local skips. But none have actually been shown to me." His head was getting worse. Daire took in a deep breath and prepared to speak.

"So they've taken this thing down to that warehouse that'll tip over if there's a little gust of wind going by?" He had meant the warehouse down at the entrance to the underground. No one ever went there, but it was rumoured to have a secret level that led underground.

"Look, no one knows that for sure! They could be doing anything down there," he looked down at Kordian who was about to interrupt again, stuck out one hand, shook his head.

"What we have to do is go down there and check. Make them stop whatever it is they're doing down there. It might have something to do with the festival. If so, we've got to stop it right now."

Worried glances were exchanged. "When?" asked Vince.

"Tonight."

Chapter Six

The Amulet

They turned round the corner into Maple Street and Beth gasped. They could see it even from the other end of the street. Xanther had been dreading this moment. Beth had known it wasn't going to be good, but it was a lot worse. She suddenly went into a sprint and Xanther followed.

"Beth! Wait!"

But she wasn't listening. The house was practically gone. "Oh God," she whispered. The fact that she had absolutely no emotion in her voice whatsoever was worrying. She just stood there, looking up at the giant heap, her gaze totally expressionless.

"Are you all right?" He rested an arm on her shoulder.

She had obviously been very poor. Ignoring him, she walked up to the burnt wood to take a closer look. Xanther followed. The smell was still bad, a burnt smell. She began climbing up the rubble, supposedly looking for something that could be saved. Once she had got to the top, realization hit her. "Look, I just want to see if there's anything worth saving and then we're out of here. No sentimental bullshit. I'm scared to death of what's followed me here".

"Help me find something. Anything, that's not burned." she said. So he did. It wasn't easy, though. Everything was black.

It occurred to him while searching, that the structure of the house may not be safe. It also occurred to him that it had been cordoned off for a reason; and that they should probably head to the police station.

"You can stay with me. You'll be safe there." He looked at her silently, to show he was serious.

"Well, thank you. Are you sure?"

"Yes, I'm sure. You're the first real person I've really talked to for years and I don't want to let you go so soon."

She looked at him, puzzled. "What do you mean?" she asked.

He shook his head. "I'm a sort of agoraphobic. I'll tell you about it later."

"You are stranger than I first thought you were."

"Thanks."

"You know, I would normally refuse your kind offer – that's just the kind of person I am – but it looks like I have no choice, doesn't it? And besides, I like you. I trust you."

Xanther pretended not to hear and went to work trying to find something of value.

"I'll look over here and you look over that side." He pointed to the furthest part of the heap. Obediently, she went. Xanther sighed to himself. What a mess. Stepping over a few planks of burnt, black wood covering a just as black-looking sofa, he saw it. At first he could only see something that shone amongst the blackened belongings, but when he approached he realised it was some sort of amulet, with beads and a neck chain. Cautiously he examined it. Strangely beautiful and dark it had caught his eye by no accident.

Beth was searching in a similar area. She had found nothing yet of great value, and in her heart, did not expect to either. In fact, she thought, this giant, burnt mess resembled her life. Just then, Xanther called her name and rushed over. He was holding something.

"Beth!" he shouted. "I found something! Some sort of jewellery – what is it?" Beth, struck silent, slowly grasped the amulet from his hand, staring at it like it was from another world.

"My Brothern amulet. I never even knew it was gone from my neck," she whispered, tears slowly building up in her eyes. Without anything to say, Xanther reached out to her, his hand resting unsurely on her arm. She was shaking, but looked steadier than he felt inside. She looked up at him, and the hug came as naturally as the daylight had that morning.

They didn't find anything else of importance at the house, but Beth was glad of what they had managed to rescue anyway.

The quietness of the streets seemed to signify some change, but he couldn't be sure of what. Their footsteps echoed and a feeling of nervousness overtook him. Beth's resilience also puzzled him. She had hardly anything left and yet she was by his side, her inner strength evident yet something dark brooded deep within her. Had it been there from the start? He knew the answer was yes.

The haunted feeling stayed with him as they walked together. *Do you feel it?* He felt like asking her. His paranoia at being outside during the daytime had obviously returned in full force, and he upped his pacing. Beth glanced at him, but kept up.

"Do you feel… anything different?" he asked her.

"What do you mean?" she stammered. She felt it too. The silence around them seemed pregnant with some sort of malevolence, and all of a sudden the abandoned streets did not seem as naturally quiet as usual; they seemed eerily silent. He felt a shiver down his spine, but looking behind him things were just as they had been. Still, he had a feeling…

"Stop," he uttered. Beth halted, and the pair froze to the spot, listening. It was then she heard it, what sounded like rushed footsteps, running. More than one pair of feet, they sounded maybe a couple of blocks away. She glanced at Xanther and knew he heard it too.

Not only did they hear the sound of running, but something else too; subtler, rhythmic, deep... like a dog on a hot day, breathing loudly. They could hear its rasping breath, getting gradually louder.

It was the scream that turned her blood to ice, and then they saw them in the distance, running.

One of the men wore a red handkerchief on his head, a large semi-automatic gun in his hand. He was followed by a second man with brown hair who looked terrified, constantly checking over his shoulder.

"We need to get out of here, now!" Xanther pulled her by the hand; it took her a couple of seconds to register before they were running faster, away from whatever was behind them. She looked back to see a third figure followed by the fourth, an unnatural shade of red seemed to colour them; blood.

"Don't look back, just run!" he gasped. Together they turned into the next street and kept going, a litany of fears flooding their minds. Xanther knew there was no time to think, his heart beat fast in his chest and it felt like it was almost going to explode, the sound of his feet blocking out the noises from behind. Was it his imagination, the low deep growling that emanated a couple of streets away? He didn't want to stop and find out.

Beth tried to keep up with him as best she could; she clutched her amulet and tried not to think of what it could be. Whatever it was back there, it wasn't anything to do with her and she didn't want to stop and think about that. Confused, she kept running.

A loud bang followed. A gunshot of some kind was most likely. Beth jumped; startled she let out a small cry.

59

"What the hell!" Xanther shouted, trying to protect Beth the best he could. Another gunshot followed and her hand reached out for his.

They ran for what felt like miles, trying to cross as much distance as they possibly could get between them. Whatever was behind had the hostility of something Xanther had never felt before. When it finally felt like they could stop, they collapsed in a narrow side street. They couldn't see many people around the area, which was neither good nor relieving. Tired and scared, they tried to catch their breath, still listening for any noise that would give away the proximity of what they'd just left behind.

Beth looked at him, fear etched in her face. He squeezed her hand, still breathing hard.

"Do you… have any idea what that was?" he asked her. She shook her head, trembling; she let out a loud sigh.

"I've never felt anything like that in my life…" she admitted. What she kept to herself, was what she had felt.

A few minutes later, when they were feeling slightly more like their normal selves, they began to discuss their next move.

"We need to get back to my apartment. We'll be safe there," Xanther told her.

Raising an eyebrow, she replied, "Yes, but for how long? I wish I knew what was happening to this place, I'm scared, Xanther." Scared of what she might have brought here, and what she had done to make herself known to Them.

"Come on, it's not safe to stay here." He helped her up and they walked quickly in the direction of his apartment.

The rest of the way there was pretty normal, filled with people going about their lives. The past twenty-four hours seemed surreal.

When they reached the apartment, Beth took one look at the mess and promptly collapsed on the sofa. He fetched her a blanket, and made some hot, sweet tea to try and revive them.

"Xanther, this is too much," she said.

"Don't worry about it," he said back. But how could she repay him? She wasn't used to taking things from people, not for herself. This worried her and made her wonder at the same time.

Xanther glanced over at Beth, shakily holding the tea cup. There was no doubt she was in shock, and what he really wanted to find out was, what she was thinking. What did she think of him?

His house was remarkably, embarrassingly messy but she didn't seem to care. She looked tired as hell.

"You need to rest," he said, standing up to leave the room.

"Xanther... don't leave me, please. There's no way I can relax enough to sleep right now."

He sighed and slowly walked over to the sofa where she lay. He kneeled down and managed a smile.

"Then I'll stay."

"Tell me about you," she said.

"Well... this is kind of difficult. You know, you're just the only real person I've been able to talk to in years. I want to look after you because you've... well, you've really brought me out of myself." She realised it must have been quite difficult for him to say that.

"What do you mean by that?" she asked, intrigued by his words.

So he told her about how he had stayed inside, all day, everyday, for so long. He told her everything that had happened in his life, about the gangs, and what had happened in town. To be honest he hadn't really felt normal in years, somehow darker, watching the world through jaded eyes. How he'd tried university and failed. He told her that that had been the last time, that he had just ever gone outside while anyone could see him, hurt him, or taunt him. Only at night. Even though the underground was now evolving into something else, he couldn't forget the memories of the past, the bomb, the fighting.

"But why?" she asked, once he had finished. "Why did they want to hurt you in the first place?" But then she already knew the answer. It was common these days. You needed a tough skin.

"I don't know. Because of the way I look, because of the way I am. Maybe none of those, maybe it was all in my mind. They killed my best friend."

"You look perfectly normal," replied Beth, looking into his deep, dark eyes like giant rock pools. Suddenly it felt like she was looking into his soul, and what she saw was beautiful.

"I've been so isolated from things. I've been wasting time. I know that now. It's no way to spend a life. I feel so vulnerable, but not with you. You helped me."

"And you lived off the Internet..." She felt intrigued by this.

"Yep. I didn't realise it then, but I was so very lonely." She sat down on the bed beside him.

After that, they were both silent for a time. "Do I really look normal?" he laughed. Thinking of everything in the past, he found it hard to believe on the outside, he was still unscarred. And maybe on the inside, the damage was healed. He didn't know that yet.

She smiled. "Yes, you look perfectly normal. What about me?"

"You're exquisite." He leaned over and kissed her. He was not completely positive that this was the best thing to do. After all he didn't want to lose her now. He wondered how something could feel so right, when nothing else did. She responded to the kiss eagerly. Slowly, softly, their lips parted and he looked at her trembling. She understood that it was not easy. She was the first woman he had kissed in a very long time, and she knew he was much stronger than he thought he was.

He looked at her, nervously, as kissing didn't really make any sense in the given situation. She kissed him back and relief filled his mind. This time, he was much more confident. He held her in his arms, his hands first going round to feel her soft, silky hair, and then moving lower down her body. She put her arms around his neck. They stayed like that for a while until, finally their kiss broke.

"Let's sleep," she said. Together they fell entwined, scared and exhausted on his bed. There was nothing unnatural about how that felt, nothing perverse or sexual in the way they lay there, slipping into a deep uninterrupted sleep. Xanther dreamt.

Hazily, the couple made their way around the thick atmosphere of the fair. They walked, holding hands, inseparable. It was a crude kind of fair, really. Things were intermixed with others; the band line, where children could walk along, went down the middle of the path Xanther and Beth were walking along now.

Xanther's gaze was occupied with the picture of her, her soft long hair trailing behind her, her delicate frame in that dress. He felt a need to protect her even at the fair. Her pale skin was illuminated under the lights, which created a strange feeling as the fair was still open-air, but the heat was confusing. What really stood out about Beth was her amulet. What had she called it? Brothern.

It shone beautifully and it was almost like nothing he had ever seen before, framing her beautiful neck and enchanting him completely. He knew, unexplainably that it was not just an amulet, it served as their protection. He knew they needed protection. A picture in his mind, a face was blocked from his view but he didn't have to look to know it was evil.

Xanther felt a sense of having done this before, but it was very slight, far away in his mind like a dream he'd had when he was a child. It was dusky evening and almost misty.

A vivid chaotic animal, Xanther thought, was how this fair seemed. Each body part was doing completely different things, joining together at parts to look completely out of place. A cart was being loaded with strange looking men in creature suits, possibly for some sort of entertainment, although the cart was in the direction of the Big Wheel.

The Big Wheel in itself, through sheer size was insane. In-between all this madness it seemed to be the pillar, holding everything together and making it concrete. Its colours intermixed, orange, pink, purple and green; it stood like a giant sentient being. Its cars had lights and the ones at the top looked like fireflies. Xanther was guided past this sight by Beth, and after having to duck a couple of times they came across the wave machine.

An older woman met them at the entrance as arranged and together all three of them stepped inside. Xanther saw at once the small sized pool and the waves. In the pool structure, there were ledges to hold onto and overhead lights. From his point of view, he could not see a lifeguard. Beth had somehow expressed great interest in riding the waves, to Xanther's great concern. Her heart somehow made her vulnerable and she was weak from her last travel. However, she could now live a normal life and his worry for her edged on beneath the surface of his expression as he watched her remove the dress to reveal a blue swimsuit underneath. Turning towards the sound of the old woman and the arrangements, he nodded in the right places.

The woman was in her early fifties, with a slightly podgy face and a dirty blonde bob that fell short of her shoulders. Her eyes were wide and friendly and her nose was slightly hook-shaped. Xanther watched as her hands waved and twirled about in conversation, her floppy yellow sleeves swishing with them. This fair was mostly down to her to plan; all he wanted was to help Beth and be her protector for life.

She was in the pool now, the waves beginning to start up. There were seven people altogether, all of them cheering for more. Beth looked happy, slightly closer to the edge of the pool than the others. He watched as the waves rose higher and higher and his heart began to pound in his chest. The waves were a lot higher than he first imagined them to be, and rising. Beth was holding her own though, perhaps a little too close to the edge for his liking.

Another wave shot up, then another in quick succession. Beth was unprepared for the second and breathed water in, causing her to cough. Another wave, another, she choked and grabbed frantically for the ledge. The other swimmers took no notice, but Xanther watched as she held on to safety.

"Oh, do you think she's all right?" The woman's concern crept into her voice, causing it to sound slightly shrill. His eyes were still on Beth, who looked to be getting her breath back, as head down she held to the ledge. They couldn't walk over as it was on the other side where no platform stood. In his heart, he registered her failure and felt pain for her.

Soon, the wave session was over and Beth was able to swim back to the platform. The woman, who was not really welcome here, handed her a towel and she quickly towelled her hair, smiling at Xanther.

Shortly, they returned to the fairground. It was slightly darker, when their feet touched the dusty ground, their hands entwined. The women browsed the stalls and Xanther watched the carnies laughing and joking.

People, all shapes and sizes now were flooding all around the grounds of the fair. The small rides were busy, and children laughed and played. The air seemed thick, like a heavy kind of atmosphere and Xanther's smile slowly faded from his face.

It was the sense of déjà vu he felt now, a feeling so terrible it twisted down in his heart. This feeling occurred when something bad was going to happen, but not normally this far ahead in time. Suddenly he glanced up to the Big Wheel at the same time as his ears were almost deafened by the loud creaks of breaking metal. He held onto Beth tightly as they watched in horror.

It happened slowly: the creaks seemed like a dream as the structure of the big wheel started to bend forward, buckling under its weight, seeming to fold over and then there was no stopping it; the wheel fell. The air seemed static, screams and voices filled the air and the couple's gaze was held by the still slightly moving wheel, the base now completely broken as if melted by the heat. The wheel was falling rapidly and hit the ground with a distorting, sickening series of sounds. It fell away from Xanther and Beth, away from the majority of the fair but still objects were destroyed and people ran towards the scene to help.

Beth was being held tightly to Xanther, as the couple looked on in horror at the unnatural scene, the wheel forever broken, like the people that were inside it. Sirens began to fill the scene with noisy alarms, and the couple stepped back further.

People were rushing past and their little world slowly began to evaporate, a scene with its solid apartness, melting into one to the sound of the whispery far away noise of the carnival music.

He awoke alone, startled and full of hollow memories from his dream. Strange, how he should dream of her, and also to know he was falling in love with her. Quickly he got up, walked through the hall to see her turn sharply towards him, clasping the amulet to her chest. She stood by the window, the moonlight shining against her pale skin. Quietly, she'd stood up from the bed and watched him sleep. He looked so vulnerable. How peacefully he slept. Slowly she'd crept out of the room, searching for her things. Fear always in the back of her mind, she felt the need to run; yet she was tired of running now. The dull ache she felt in her heart only increased. She'd gathered up her small amount of possessions when she noticed him standing there.

"Where are you going?" His eyes met hers and slowly she placed the amulet on the table.

"Nowhere," she sighed. Looking down, she didn't know where she was thinking of running, but something made her want to get away. Defeated, she knew she had to stay there with him. Something stopped her from telling him her fear that 'They' may have entered her life once more.

"I need a shower, and some fresh clothes," she told him. He nodded; it'd been a long day that just kept getting stranger.

"I dreamt about you," he said. This made her laugh, shakily, but it was definitely a laugh.

"Just one day and we're already dreaming of each other," she replied, in good humour. He never did get to find out what happened in her dream.

Chapter Seven

The Portal

The white-coated figure sat at the desk, vaguely aware he was surrounded by dimming lights and paperwork that was not his. He picked up the phone that sat beside him, and slowly dialled a number before letting the receiver rest on his ear.

Behind the proofed glass lay a scattering of corpses that had once been Steifler's team. Pools of blood coloured what was once the white floor of the lab. Inside the receiver, the phone was ringing.

"Wolf, the first test is complete," Steifler spoke softly into the phone.

"The result?" A rough voice answered him through the receiver.

"It's… the hole is getting bigger. I don't know how to stop it, I can't stabilise it." Steifler's disconnected voice continued, "It's got a pull to it…"

There was silence down the line, as Steifler stared at the large mass of colour so out of place in the no-longer air-tight room.

"I'm coming," came the growl, followed by a dead line. Steifler absently put down the receiver, his attention still focused on the portal ahead of him. His eyes seemed to grow sleepy as he watched the almost hypnotising array of colours that drew him like a moth.

Angrily, he snapped out of the peaceful state, grabbing the papers on his desk and scrunching them up into balls before slamming his fist on the wooden table.

He had realised the thing was able to play tricks on him, make his mind wander. He was aware of its evil; even now he felt its pull from behind the glass. He cursed the lab under his breath as he stood to make his coffee; he turned and walked out the door into the laboratory.

The white of his soft shoes turned to red as the blood seeped in. He stepped closer to the portal. It stared at him, taunting him to go further. He dropped the plastic cup to the floor.

Subconsciously, his hands reached out as if to touch the bright painful mass that grew before him and he found himself moving closer to it.

It was as if he was outside of his body, watching the bloodstained walls of the lab, the bodies of his fellow team below him scattered on the floor. He saw himself, walking closer and closer to the rip in the dimension they had created. There was nothing he could do. He watched completely paralyzed to stop what was about to happen.

He felt it. Cold it bit through his fingertips and suddenly he was back in first person, feeling himself being sucked deep into the unknown. He could see further than he'd ever wanted to see, into places he'd never dreamed of finding. He tried to scream, but no sound would escape his lips.

The lab was left empty, the portal without company.

It was now 7:00 pm. It was another dark night, black with no stars in sight. Vincent Cullen ran down the alleyway, leading up to the far side of the warehouse. The others were waiting there for him. The snow had started again about forty five

69

minutes ago and now it fell down in light little flakes, making him more aware of the danger of slipping. Vincent didn't mind. Snow was the least of his worries.

He jogged round the corner to see four dark, but familiar figures, crouched near one of the windows.

"Hey, I'm back. I couldn't see anything, no sign." Vincent said in a breathless, exhausted voice. He had been told to go around the other side, climb onto the roof and look down through the glass part of the ceiling to get a better view. This was perhaps a stupid plan considering it involved one so clumsy.

Sam stood up. This was what he had been expecting. "Well then," he sighed. "You know what we're going to have to do now, don't you?"

The gang exchanged worried glances with one another. They had been dreading this, to actually go inside the building and get directly in possible contact with some cult psychos.

The warehouse itself had been built into the outskirts of the underground system, and was actually an old storage vault that had been in use around two hundred years ago. The warehouse itself was built on ground level, the trick being the secret floors beneath led to the vaults.

It was a trader's secret, known only to a few people, yet somehow Raoul and friends had managed to claim this as their own.

A fresh faced, clean-clothed Xanther sat in the living room, eyeing the bottle of vodka on the table with contempt. This evening was going to be interesting. Beth had told him she needed to get in contact with some guys she knew, who might be able to help her out. The best way to do this would be to go underground, to the old systems that he'd once known as a teenager.

She'd assured him it had changed a lot since then, that it was safe and quite a friendly place. In fact, most of the trouble happened above ground these days. Still, he felt nervous at the prospect of remembering ghosts of the past. *Come on, you might even see someone you know,* she'd said.

Just then the bedroom door creaked open, and Beth emerged. Along with her jeans, she'd been able to do something with one of his old t-shirts, and a pair of scissors. How she'd managed to look that great, he couldn't really work out but it made him smile.

"Hello, stranger," she smiled back.

"Are we ready to go?" he replied. She nodded, taking in another glance of the messy room and sitting next to him on the sofa. She turned to him casually.

"Got any weapons?" Beth asked. He just looked at her, blankly. She laughed. "You know, just in case."

I might have," he replied with a worried look.

"You know that the underground festival, Mallia is only a couple of days away and there might be some trouble. You know the underground was originally gang territory and even though most of the fighting is over there's still a feeling of hostility between groups."

"Yeah I've heard of Mallia, I don't know why they still go ahead with it," said Xanther.

"I came to this town a year and a half ago, the underground welcomed Luke and I and we... I mean I... probably wouldn't be here now otherwise," she told him. It was the truth; she'd been young and scared, fleeing the way she'd had to all her life. She stood up.

"Oh, I almost forgot; my amulet," she said, throwing it over her neck. She looked ready for anything, Xanther thought.

Feeling better and armed with Xanther's switch blade, Beth was ready to go. Leaving the apartment was like leaving a warm comfort blanket behind. They were reminded of what happened earlier, the breathing and the blood.

It didn't take long for the cold to hit them; the light snow blew through Beth's hair as they walked under the starless sky. The buildings around them were mostly dark and quiet, almost as if they were sleeping.

He knew the way, but he let her lead him to the seal. It'd been a long time since he'd been underground, but he remembered the main seal as if it was burnt into his mind, a tortured memory.

The largest seal around the underground is known as the main gate, guarded by civilians and kept closed off. This was merely a precaution; entering was easy, but if need be all the seals could also be locked at any time, preventing those inside from getting out. The south gate was the second largest seal and lay at the south of Middletown. The main gate was to the west; it was here Xanther and Beth approached now, together and shrouded by snow.

The seal was decorated by an emblem of the fighter, etched into the metallic surface; the seal was made out of reinforced steel.

The pair entered, nodded to the cloaked guard who smiled at them; hostility was not the name of the game anymore. Ahead of them was a dimly lit corridor, but wide with high ceilings and plenty of space. It was almost possible to forget where you were, apart from the darkness and basic ceilings that built the character of the place.

Despite this, the place seemed full of life. Music beat freely and they were greeted by many stalls and people, all part of the underground system that brought life to the dying town of Middletown. The variety of punters who walked through the systems was amazing, and Xanther admired their bright clothes of luxurious fabrics, their punk hairstyles, the PVC clad youths and the Goths; luscious darklings who wore clothes of velvet, satin and lace, their pale faces and dark make-up shiny under the dim lights.

72

Beth seemed relaxed and happier here, as if the worry of the outside had melted away by the music and vibe that presented itself. It was evident the festival was only days away, with notices and offers posted on the walls.

They slowly made their way through the crowd. Beth smiled at him and for the first time, took his hand in hers, pulling him deeper into the crowd of strangers. Somewhere up ahead, a band played, the singer echoing through the elaborate pathways, her voice soothing and unnatural to his ears.

He passed a tall skinny man dressed in hippy trousers and bright waistcoat, his hair bright orange and a tattoo down one side of his face, a blue tribal print. His contact lenses shone bright, almost metallic looking.

A round elegant woman was tending her stall of elaborate silver jewellery, and he stopped to look. She smiled kindly.

"Moonstone," she said. "Is an exquisite stone, meant to be most beautiful under the light of the moon. This ring is the one for your girly, sir." Xanther smiled back, slightly perturbed but at the same time curious. Beth had stopped and stood beside him, looking at the necklaces and bracelets.

"Xanther we need to find those guys," she looked at him.

"I'll take it," he said. He bought the ring, and slipped it onto her finger. She gave him a 'not impressed' look, and then laughed, took him by the hand and made as if to drag him forwards.

The complicated underground network had been disused for around a couple of hundred years, long before there was any sign of trouble in Middletown.

The couple wandered through the bright colours of the crowd, Xanther being led by a determined and noticeably more confident Beth, counting each unit as they walked by.

The Cullens normally occupied Unit 28, as it was marked; this was where they held their base but not their home.

The concrete around them looked brighter than Xanther remembered: it seemed so long ago that he and Andrew had walked these underground pathways, so long ago that so much death seeped through the very walls they were able to reach out and touch now.

Beth seemed to sense his unease and firmly squeezed his hand, shot him a glance and turned a corner, avoiding the many brightly clothed people who had noticed them.

Beth was looking all around now, as if she was trying to find someone in particular. They approached a small eatery when he heard her all of a sudden shout, "Uncle!"

He turned and she was jumping and waving at an elderly gentleman who got up from his chair, a smile across his face.

"Sweet Cub!" the old man called back, arms outstretched.

Beth let go of Xanther's hand and embraced 'Uncle' while he stood awkwardly in the doorway. The eatery was lit up with candles and bright red and gold canvasses lined the walls. An elegant rug adorned the floor covered in luxuriant fabrics, cushions and very low but comfortable looking seats. A sign above the bar read 'Garvelia The Red'.

Beth announced, "This is Uncle, a man very close to my own heart." The old man smiled at Xanther before making a small bow.

Xanther, a bemused look on his face also bowed back, and Uncle laughed.

"Dear children, sit down and make yourselves comfortable. I shall prepare some of my special Jhaki tea." Uncle's voice enchanted Xanther and he found himself sitting down next to Beth.

Beth confided, "I used to work for Uncle. I call him that because he's as close to family as I get these days."

Xanther nodded, his eyes were once again drawn to Uncle. The elderly gentleman was rather pale of face, but not sallow, with red cheeks and what appeared to be no hair apart from a single white braid under his delicately sewn hat. He was quite short, with elaborately woven robes that looked foreign. Xanther could not place Uncle's accent but it sounded strange to his Middlish ears.

Uncle handed the pair two strangely cube-shaped warm mugs and sat down across from them, the smile never wavering from his face.

"So, my darling, what can be done for you today? I have missed you; you need to visit more often!" spoke Uncle.

"I am sorry, Uncle, but I have been far too pre-occupied with my own troubles and do not wish to pollute the Red with my words. But there's something going on in the town and I don't like it."

Uncle took a breath and looked solemn for a second, "Yes, I know of something which has become deeply unsettled. I know of your problems also. You are searching for the Cullens, no?" Beth nodded, "I knew you'd understand."

As Xanther sipped his sweet drink, he became aware of the deep bond Uncle and Beth shared, as if they were almost father and daughter.

Uncle had been talking of the deep unrest which had come to be out in the open, and the underground's horror finds which had been discovered in the last couple of months when he said, "It is becoming a dangerous place here, Beth. There is something I cannot quite place and I think it is something to do with you."

Beth's expression changed to one of acceptance, "I know... that's what I'm afraid of." One solitary tear slowly dripped down her cheek, and Uncle gently took her hand.

"I wish I knew more, I wish I could help in some way. I... wish you could tell me," Xanther finally spoke up, although what he was saying sounded so out of place and awkward. It was obvious he did not understand.

Beth sighed, her voice lowered, she turned to him. "You have to understand that I'm not from here. I have been followed for a long time and I need to stay strong for a reason. You need not get involved any further because you don't know what you are getting involved in."

"I'm not leaving you," stated Xanther, although his mind was already filling with confusion over what Beth was trying to say.

Uncle turned to him, "Boy, you are a good soul. Look after her, please. She is haunted."

"Thank you, Uncle," said Beth, looking relieved yet slightly drained.

"I will pray for you both." Uncle bowed his head once more and Xanther knew he meant it with the greatest sincerity. His second statement was meant with just as much sincerity.

"Now, you must eat well."

The restaurant was one of the few decent ones left in the area, as most were going out of business. More and more people were beginning to leave Middletown and the place was getting more deserted every day or seemed to. *It's beginning to look like a dead town,* thought Xanther.

Still, the people wealthy enough to afford to dine started to crowd the room and brought in a welcome atmosphere. Two men sat in one corner, discussing business while dressed in expensive suits. They sipped wine and looked over papers concerning stock markets. The three booming computer hardware businesses were mainly set up around a 30 mile radius of Middletown, and a lot of people who had been sacked because of a lot of local firms going bankrupt were now moving on to work in technology and computing.

Xanther read the news but wasn't sure what to believe anymore; what was manufactured slop and what was real. Middletown was being targeted by the government for new schemes encouraging youngsters away from gang activity and back into work, but training took time and money.

Anyway, people needed to work and staying in Middletown wasn't really an option for a lot of people because there were limited jobs and no real opportunity anymore, at least above ground. People were being made redundant because of bad business, and the bad business was mainly because of the town's reputation. The gangs and the fighting, the homeless and the general decline of the town didn't help matters. It was like it was receding into something less than a town. It was slowly dying.

Xanther brought his thoughts back to Beth. She looked up at him and smiled, and for a moment, everything was so perfect. She thought he must be as nervous as she was, before looking back down at her hands.

Beth was having trouble working him out. He didn't seem to be comfortable in The Red, like in the same way he didn't seem to be too comfortable with people. She wondered if it was her that he wasn't comfortable with, and if she was comfortable with him. Yes, she was. Her thoughts were broken when an argument broke out beside them. Some punks were thrown out by a much younger looking, taller version of Uncle, wearing the same elaborate clothes and shoes.

The old man had gotten up to serve the newcomers and make sure everyone ate well, including Xanther and Beth.

The warmth grew when the small fireplace was lit and Xanther found himself looking into the flames with a smile on his face; being with Beth, no matter what the circumstances, meant that he was happy, ridiculously happy. He was just waiting for the downfall to start creeping into his mind. He held her hand and Uncle looked over, a deep calm and happiness seemed to emanate from within him.

Chapter Eight

The Awakening

The group of dark figures entered stealthily, through the broken window of the old underground warehouse. Vincent was scared; his hands were shaking as he climbed in last. He almost lost his footing as a bit of broken glass cracked underneath him, causing him to jump and lose his balance. All of the men heard the noise as he hit the floor, causing them all to freeze.

"Shit!" whispered Vincent. The group stood there frozen for about half a minute, wondering if they had been heard. It was very dark, but the large room was empty and Sam didn't think there was much to see.

"Right OK… I think it's safe to keep going." whispered Sam. Vince opened his mouth to say something, but before any word could be formed, he was interrupted by a huge bloodcurdling scream – a woman's scream – coming from below them.

"Oh fuck…" said Sam.

"It sounded like they're killing her. Sam, we have to do something," Vincent whispered, secretly terrified. There was another scream, longer this time, somehow more pained. It didn't sound nice. Daire wanted out and said so.

"Come on, we've got to see what they're doing down there..." said Sam, convincing himself to move forward. Vince followed then Daire, then Kordian and Marcus who took up the back. Their footsteps made tiny sounds on the concrete floor, but as the screaming was becoming more frequent, they weren't going to be heard.

They approached the other side of the room and stood by the door, planning what to do next.

"Shit, I don't like this at all..." Daire whispered, echoing the thoughts of the other members. His voice sounded shaky, nervous. His black hair shone in the moonlight. Sam brought his fingers to his mouth making a 'shhhh' sound, then beckoning with his hands to open the door. Vincent shook his head violently; he sensed something was not right down there.

"Right, what do you suggest we do Vince? Stand here all night doing fuck all!" whispered Sam. Vincent and the other members stared back, silent but scared.

"Come on, follow me," Sam told them.

Kordian and Daire shrugged. Vincent looked worried, asking his question, "What if they see us? I don't want to see what they're doing!" The sounds were still going strong, cutting through the stale air of the warehouse like a knife. Daire shivered.

"Look, we've got to do something; *somebody* has to – what the fuck? Listen!" Sounds of something else, something alive and terrible filled the air; drowning out the woman's screams and making the five of them stand still. It sounded like a sort of animal. Marcus looked terrified, his legs all of a sudden felt like rubber.

"Shit! I want out of here. It's not safe!" Vincent said. Sam shook his head, but Vincent was right. He was not so much afraid of who was down there, just what he didn't understand. The scream started to taper off, and then stopped abruptly. The five men looked around at each other; all five faces had the same expression, utter fear.

"Let's get out! She's dead, she must be, so let's get out, before…" whispered Marcus, who had been mostly quiet until now.

"They won't kill us, and yes, I think she's dead too." answered Sam.

"What did they do to her…?" asked Vince in a whisper. Nobody answered. Just then they heard noises seeming to be ascending stairs. They heard two, maybe three people's voices, and footsteps, coming closer.

"Fuck this; let's get out of this place!"

"There's no time. We have to hide," Sam ran towards a vehicle near the corner of the room and the others followed. They all hid behind some sort of vehicle, hidden under a huge tarp of canvas. Sam blamed himself for not thinking the plan out clearly. He hoped they hadn't heard anything. If they had, the outcome wouldn't be pretty.

Back at the Red, Xanther and Beth were talking over sweet Jhaki tea. The night had been an eye-opener for Xanther, and Beth now looked a little sad. He cared about her, thought maybe they should start heading back soon – so she could get some sleep, but she had insisted on ordering some more tea first to awaken her senses.

"Xanther, I want to ask you about something…"

"Yeah, go ahead," he smiled, patiently.

"You know the town? As a whole? Does it seem any different to you?" She looked straight into his black eyes as she asked the question, and he looked right back at her.

"What do you mean, 'different'?"

"I don't feel safe here anymore. Something is happening here, I feel sure of it. Something… bad."

"Bad?" he looked perplexed. She knew this wasn't a good idea, mentioning it here.

"It's just; things have been going on at night. I hear screams sometimes, and the way there seem to be less and less people around everyday, worries me," she explained.

He knew what she meant. He had heard screaming too, and he was sure he'd seen a few strange shapes following him when he went for walks at night, but he wasn't about to scare her.

"I know, things can seem a little scary when you are on your own at night. Don't worry, I'll always be here with you now. I won't leave." He smiled. She smiled slightly too, but it looked forced. "Don't worry, I think something might be going on too, but I think it's more to do with gangs than anything else. And what you've been through, no wonder you're worried."

"Yeah, I guess so," she replied, looking slightly more relieved now, although a shadow still seemed to darken her eyes. He reached out his hand to her, and she took it. "You won't leave me, will you?"

"No."

They five guys crouched down as silent as possible, as they heard voices and footsteps getting nearer. The door opened, and dark figures entered the large room. Two of them appeared to be carrying something, wrapped in cloth.

"Hurry up; we weren't exactly fucking silent in there!" Sam recognised that deep voice. It was Neil; one of the guys he thought might have been behind this. It meant something very weird was going on.

"Yeah, she put up a fight, but is supplying it with energy. Really what it needs…" said another voice.

Another man, sounding agitated said, "Shut up and get her into the truck. We can't afford to be late, we shouldn't even fucking be here and if he finds out…" No one else spoke. All they could hear were noises and Sam realised they were opening the truck, loading something into the back. Vincent looked apprehensively at Sam, then Daire, then Marcus. His eyes never met Kordian's, as his gaze was fixed on where the noises were coming from.

"We have to move, otherwise they'll see us," whispered Daire. They all knew that already, as they looked around for somewhere to go. Sam motioned to get under the truck itself.

"No way! The–" Vincent whispered back, but was interrupted by Sam.

"Get under there! Kordian, you and I will go round the front when they get in. Get really low down. Crawl if you have to. They won't see us. They're too high up."

The men seemed to be checking something, one of them violently slammed down the end of the truck. The sheer size of the vehicle meant that Vincent and the others could not be seen by the gang unless they suspected they were being watched.

Then they heard another voice, a woman's this time, "Right, all's clear, we need to move it now, boys." None of them recognised this voice, which was intelligent and stony and some of them frowned slightly. Vince, Marcus and Daire crawled under the truck keeping as low as possible and praying for the best, whilst Sam and Kordian waited for them all to get in the vehicle until they crawled down low in front. The engine started up, and they quickly managed to jump out of the way before the large truck ran them down.

They tried to pay the bill but Uncle would not accept their money. As Beth was unable to find out where the Cullens had gone, the pair got ready to walk back to Xanther's apartment. To him, she looked tired still, although she insisted she was fine. Xanther left the young-Uncle waiter a tip, then helped Beth stand. The restaurant was almost deserted now, and the music played softly in the background. They worked their way out of the vibrant pathways and left via the seal they came in by, out to the dimly lit street. It was darker now, and some of the street lamps had been broken long ago and never been repaired. Beth shivered, and Xanther brought her closer to him, as they walked further down the street and across a deserted road. There was hardly any traffic at all tonight. A cat crossed in front of them.

They passed more buildings, as they walked along past the warehouse Xanther thought he heard a noise. He stopped for a minute, and Beth looked at him, questioningly. *It's nothing,* he said to himself. He was just about to start moving again, when they first heard a loud engine noise, then a huge crash, as it drove wildly through the rotting wood of the warehouse wall. Xanther jumped back, taking hold of Beth and pulling her out of harm's way. The large truck seemed not to notice them, as it sped away down the side street at an incredible pace.

"What was *that* all about?" exclaimed Beth, when the truck was out of sight and she'd had a chance to catch her breath.

"I don't know exactly," Xanther replied, eyes fixed on the small road the lorry had shot down just a minute before. Suddenly, five men ran out of the space in the wall the truck had made, making Beth jump again. The men were breathing hard and looking wildly about as to which direction the truck had gone. Xanther wondered what had been going on in what looked like a deserted place to cause so much excitement.

One of the men seemed to recognise Beth.

"Beth! Haven't seen you since..." Sam trailed off. "Hey, are you all right?"

Beth looked at Sam, the man she recognised as one of her brother's friends.

"Sam? What the hell is going on around here?" she asked. "You scared me half to death!"

"Don't ask me. We need to follow that truck." Vincent walked up to them, looking puzzled.

"Man, we almost got caught behind that truck! If they had seen us... Where do you think they're going?"

"Where did who go?" asked Beth.

"We're not sure but we think it was the guys who killed…" He didn't have to say any more, her face said it all.

"T-t-they went th-th-that way." She pointed in the direction the large truck had gone. Xanther saw that Sam looked as sad as Beth did. "Tell me, what were you doing in there? With them!"

"We just came down to check it out, heard a girl screaming down there and we think she's dead." Sam hung his head. Vince looked awkwardly at the rest of the gang, then at Xanther.

"Who are you?" Vincent asked.

"This is Xanther. He's with me," answered Beth. She instinctively reached out for Xanther's hand, and he squeezed hers, reassuringly.

"Well, hey, why don't we meet up again soon? Real soon. I want to ask you some things; anything you might know could help us. Something is going on here and it's not good." Sam shook his head.

Just then, a dustbin fell to the ground, making everyone jump. Beth gasped, squeezed Xanther's hand.

"OK," said Sam, "Whoever's behind there, come out slowly and we won't hurt you."

Nothing, complete silence from the bins. Then, a small figure emerged and came into the light, followed by a smaller figure who started to pant.

"Freya what have we told you…" sighed Vincent. "What the hell are you doing here! You could have gotten hurt." The dog was now at Vincent's side, and he patted it, reassuringly. All five brothers stared accusingly at their nine year old sister, Freya.

"Freya, have you been following as again?" asked Sam, patiently.

"No, I swear. I was taking Brett's dog out for a walk, and I saw you go in there!" She pointed to the warehouse. "So I hid, to

84

see what you were doing. Sammy, that lady screaming scared me… is she really dead?"

Sam sighed, Marcus looked at her sorrowfully. "Well honey, I don't know," said Marcus. "It's very dangerous for you to be out on your own at this time of night, and you shouldn't be spying on us either."

"I'm sorry. I had Yemmie with me. He protects me!" she said. "I was scared, so I hid…"

"That's okay, babe. Why don't we get you home now, huh? You must be cold," said Sam, taking her hand in his and giving Daire a worried glance as he did so.

Xanther told the brothers it was okay for them to drop by tomorrow, so they could try and figure out the puzzle. These were old friends of Beth's and it seemed like they needed her help. Marcus and Kordian then escorted Freya home, while the others ran back into the night, looking for an answer.

On the way back to Xanther's apartment, Beth once again spoke of what was going on in Middletown. Maybe her brother's friends had something to do with it? Maybe they could help.

"It sounds like they're trying hard to get to the bottom of whatever is going on around here," Xanther said. "It looks like it involves the other gang. I think Sam's on our side." He looked at her to see her reaction, but she seemed fine. She looked back at him, and he knew he was already too far involved to unravel himself now.

When they got back to the apartment, they both sat on her bed. Beth yawned, she looked exhausted.

"I'm worried, Xanther," she said.

"I know. Don't be worried. I'll look after you."

She looked at him. "What if I don't want looking after? I've been looking after myself for long enough. Maybe I should be the one looking after you."

He excused himself to the bathroom, and she got into bed, struck by the coldness of the room. By the time Xanther got back, she was fast asleep. He got in beside her, held her as she stirred a little. "Xanther?" She asked, sleepily.

"Yes, it's me. I'm not leaving you tonight." As he kissed her on the cheek, he could feel her heartbeat and he wrapped his arms protectively around her fragile body. The pair slept, enveloped in each other.

Chapter Nine

Orders

Raoul kicked the wall angrily. Neil and Timmon looked on in contempt as they waited for Vesrah to return, knowing the Wolf would not be pleased with their actions; he didn't seem like the sort of man to take bad news well. Timmon felt there was something deeply wrong about their new leader, but couldn't dare speak the words. An untraceable fear seemed to enter his mind but the train of thought never really left the station.

Vesrah had her charms; she thought she was close to the Wolf. Raoul didn't trust that one bit, knowing she'd probably be the first one to get thrown aside if the plan failed.

When they managed to capture one of the beasts, they restrained it in one of the top rooms of the warehouse. Unsure of what it could do they'd fed it the best they could using live supplies, waiting on their commissioner's instruction. From the feeding, its mass had somehow grown and they did not know how long they'd be able to control it.

The second beast remained at large despite their best efforts. It had proved too powerful to be taken down with bullets and it had almost eaten one of them; it was stronger than they had predicted. Now Raoul's left arm was heavily bandaged.

The Wolf, stranger than Raoul had first thought, was secretive. It was obvious he had his own intentions; he thought, why the hell would he want to trust the guy. Deep down he knew he didn't exactly have a choice anymore.

Once again, the gang had been reckless; afraid of being caught, they had left Beth deep in the flames where she had in turn been rescued. As far as they knew, she was supposed to be dead.

"Neil," Timmon told him, "From what we know he could be as angry as hell, and he doesn't look like a nice kind of guy."

It had been days since they had heard from the Wolf, his bitter voice instructing them where to find the bombs. It was then they had begun their new roles as terrorists, something that seemed good enough to trust.

They had put the bombs together unprofessionally and desperately, clumsy in their impatience. The bombs in turn had been placed under the walkways for the festival and were ready for detonation. But for the next few days they would sleep peacefully, deep underground.

All the terrorists could do now was lie low and watch the pandemonium, waiting for the Wolf to return to the den.

Xanther found himself immersed in a large space. A large purple space? *What is that colour?* In leaked blues and reds turning into the most vibrant orange, that looking at it seemed to burn his eyes. He was floating *(floating in space)* through some purple *(what is that colour?)* space. Only the air had substance, but he could still breathe. It felt velvety in his fingers, comforting but strange *(floating in time? What is that colour?)* and he didn't know where he was. He didn't care, it was all so beautiful and it relaxed him. The world around him seemed to be filled with colour, but colour he had never *(what is that colour?)* seen before in his life. Colour he couldn't seem to determine. It seem to be changing all the time, so it was more like green, then

88

red, but not quite *(purple?)* and he couldn't work it out. He seemed to be floating around; comfortable in this wonderful texture of golds and colours he didn't know. He didn't seem to be going anywhere, and he relaxed as he marvelled at all the beautiful colours. The orange had stopped hurting his eyes by now, and it was amazing to look at, flashing in and out like a beating heart. It felt alive. All of a sudden, he felt he was gently being pulled in one direction, backwards. There was a feeling he at first could not bring himself to recognise, then all at once, as he started to turn to see where he was headed, he knew. It was dread, fear, terror. As he turned around – as quickly as it could allow him to – he saw THE colour. He couldn't define what colour it was, but it was a horrible colour. It made his heart stop in his chest and his blood freeze. It is completely new to him, this feeling he felt, but it was the worst feeling he had ever experienced in his life. He opened his mouth to scream, when all of a sudden...

He found himself in a dull, grey world. Looking up at the sky, his back against the hot ash ground he saw something unexplainable in the sky.

It looked like a dead thing, skeletal and at odd angles it flapped and cawed above him. Around it was a mass of red sky, blotted with black across the landscape.

He saw trees that looked like they had died long ago, black and ashy, devoid of fluid. The air tasted hot and dry and noises startled him, filling the sky.

He could hear the shrieking as if from someone who'd clearly gone insane, only there was no way the noise could be coming from anything that was possibly human.

He was finding it difficult to breathe, the air growing increasingly hot around him. Standing up he saw nothing for miles, apart from dead trees and black sand.

He could feel his body was drenched in sweat as he started to gasp for air; it seemed to be getting thicker around him, making it harder to breath.

A large purple moon seemed to glare down at him as he fell to his hands and knees, clasping at his throat.

It was then he realised he was going to die in the alien world, surrounded by nothingness. The shrieks seemed to get louder, more powerful as if suggesting his death was awaiting.

His chest began to hurt and his skin started to burn, his eyes unseeing as he fell against the ash. Everything turned white and he felt a surge of colour, before he woke up in bed with a start.

Beth lay next to him and gently she hugged herself closer to him as he realised his skin was dry. She felt soft against his arms as he slipped back into sleep.

The next morning, Beth awoke to find the room bathed in rays of sunlight. She lay there, in the warm bed, and looked at what surrounded her. *Pretty room,* she thought. Very pretty. The room itself wasn't pretty at all; it was terribly messy yet it seemed to encase Xanther's personality perfectly. Things seemed to lie in a well-constructed mess that only one person could understand. She turned to this one person now, who lay sleeping beside her, his beautifully carved face a sight she was still not used to. She was glad not to have woken up here alone, and the night before had been special. Now she lay awake next to this special person, she lay silently to watch him sleep.

After a few minutes, he opened his eyes to see her peacefully smiling at him, as she lay beside him in the small, unkempt bed. He looked like some version of a dark angel sleeping here, and she was glad to see him open those wonderful dark eyes, to look at her adoringly.

She kissed him, and nothing else mattered. Nothing else in the world mattered, and there was no untidy little room, no bed, no furniture and no world outside of their embrace, just them.

They kissed for a long time, just kissing, tasting each other with an innocent kind of curiosity, so pleasant, so sensual. Then he gently moved his hand down from where he had been stroking her hair, until it softly fell on her breast, making her jump ever so slightly, in a pleasurable way. It made her heart skip a beat, and she felt him caressing her there, first very gently, then more thoroughly. The kissing was now more passionate, and she was now more aware that she was still wearing her dress from the night before. Lovingly, Xanther started to lift it up, over her head and then it was on the floor, and soon they were both completely naked. He kissed her first on the lips, then down her neck, down her chest to her breasts. She moaned softly in pleasure, and he wanted her so badly. He pulled her on top of him, and she looked down at him, her eyes loving, his own glazed with lust. She felt herself melt as their tongues caressed each other, him on top of her now. They made love and it was like slipping into heaven. They both moaned as the pleasure started to turn into ecstasy, and as their beat got quicker and harder. She cried out, and they both came together, as if they were one being. Xanther collapsed on top of her, both of them breathless, sweaty and spent.

"I think I love you," he told Beth, twenty minutes later when they had got their breath back. They were now lying side by side in bed; the room took on an entirely different quality. He felt great, embraced in her love and she looked so beautiful now, so radiant. He kissed her on the cheek.

"I think I love you too," she said, smiling that wonderful smile of hers. She didn't really understand what was happening, but she kept those thoughts to herself; *how could she be capable of love after all that had happened to her?*

It was now 09:25 am. Beth stood up, and walked naked to the bathroom, as Xanther looked at her, with a dumbstruck expression on his face.

Beth looked at herself in the mirror and for once was happy with what she saw. She smiled, washed her hands and ventured back out into the room they had slept in. The thought made her smile. *I love him.*

She wasn't given the chance to ask about breakfast, as he had already grabbed her in his arms and lifted her back into bed. He'd never been this intimate with anyone, probably *ever.* It was wonderful. He felt so happy, just to be so close to her. He realised he loved her much more than he could have ever thought possible. How could this have happened?

Chapter Ten

The Meeting/Marcus

The group assembled in the small apartment. It was now early afternoon. Sam was sitting in a chair near the corner, but all eyes were on him as he recounted the tale of last night. Vincent, Kordian and Daire sat around him. Marcus hadn't shown up.

He told of the screams and the noises that had started coming from below, and then of the footsteps and how lucky they had been not to get caught. Vincent interrupted every now and then with "Damn right we did!" or "Yeah! Fucking weird, man!" but Beth's gaze never left Sam's, and he focused most of his attention on her. Xanther was holding her hand in his; he could see how troubled Sam's eyes looked. And the dark bags under his eyes showed how little he had slept last night.

"So, you're saying they are doing this for the same reasons they killed Luke?" asked Beth, slowly and with deliberate effort, but not avoiding the words this time.

Sam lowered his head, "Yes," he said. He looked at her now, "Look Beth, we didn't know. I'm sorry, there wasn't anything we could do."

"I know Sam, I know. There's no point looking back now, is there?" Beth was still looking at Sam, but her eyes were filling up with tears, and it wasn't so long before she had to look away again. "Excuse me, I'm going to the bathroom," she said, getting up. Xanther looked at Sam, then Vince.

"So, these guys are dangerous?"

"In a word, yes," said Sam.

"We don't know how much, but something must be driving them," said Vincent, pretty much his normal self today. Xanther sighed; he was beginning to get worried. An irrational thought entered his mind, that perhaps it was something to do with the bad feeling he'd had – *what is that colour* – but suddenly the thought was lost.

Beth entered the room a couple of minutes later, to find Xanther with a confused but slightly agitated look on his face. "What's wrong?" she asked, putting a hand on his shoulder.

"Who was Luke?" He turned to look at her.

She turned away immediately and silence filled the room; he sensed that tears had filled her eyes before she uttered the words, "He was my brother."

Sam's eyes narrowed at Xanther and he asked Beth harshly, "Where did you meet this guy?"

She turned to him, astonished at his words. "I met him when he saved my life," her voice shakily raised. She saw his expression suddenly ashamed.

Marcus, the middle child, had decided to give the party a miss. Well, he thought, it was hardly a party. Although they never really got along, he had known Luke, and felt sad for Beth, but he expressed no desire to tell her his best wishes. He had something else in mind.

He found himself outside the warehouse, before he stepped inside the hole that the truck had conveniently made the night before.

The place looked totally different in the daylight he thought, almost eerily different. Now, it was only a large room with a concrete floor, not scary at all. Not even the dark spots, as the daylight came through the hole in the wall and through the very few windows. He sighed; this was not exactly the cult haven he had expected. Although no doubt, the amateurs had probably left a few clues behind.

He'd come here for precisely that reason, to look for some sort of clue. It was like something was summoning him here, like, he was meant to be here. He stopped; a thought had come into his head. Not a nice one. He'd dreamt the night before, and he was sure it hadn't been nice. Oh well, it was closed to him now. He walked further down the room, towards the door.

He found himself shivering. It wasn't a cold day, but somehow he had caught a draught. He was getting closer to the door now, and he was starting to have second thoughts; completely irrational and very annoying to his usually rational mind. He might find something…unpleasant. *I have to do this for Luke, and for us,* he thought.

In one swift movement, he opened the door and took a step inside the inner building.

The stairs were darker than he'd hoped, and they creaked when he stepped on one. They were made of old wood, which meant he would have to be careful. Half-heartedly testing each step before he trusted his weight on it, he made his uncertain way down the stairs. Halfway down, the door shut behind him. The steps were longer than he thought, and the staircase was getting narrower. He noticed there were steps going upwards too, which was strange as he did not know of an attic. He thought maybe he should check those out after, although if there was an attic, it couldn't be very big.

He neared the bottom of the stairs, and saw that there was a light on down there. He listened, but the room was completely silent, so stealthily, he ventured in. The room was lit by one single bulb, hanging from the high ceiling. Apart from that, it was dark and shadows lurked in the corners of the room. Looking around, Marcus could see a single chair, nothing else.

Slightly disappointed (but secretly relieved), he let out a long sigh. Everything seemed normal down there, apart from that light, maybe –

He froze. There was a creak on the stairs, near the top. There no mistaking the sound, as he had just came down those stairs himself. He was frozen on the spot, listening intently. All he could hear was his heartbeat, no more creaks to indicate someone was actually on their way down, whoever it was. His heart was thumping in his chest, but he made himself move forward, back to the staircase.

The stairs twisted round at the bottom, so he couldn't see much. He stopped and listened for something else. Nothing. After what seemed like a couple of minutes, he began to calm down. He started to walk slowly up the staircase. *Had that smell been there a minute ago*, he thought to himself. Strange that he hadn't noticed until now. It smelled of something rotten, he couldn't quite describe…

Another creak. Marcus's heart jumped up in his chest, before he realised it had been him that had made that creak. He could now see up the staircase, and there was nobody there. *Nobody, nothing, no, Sir.* But the attic…the staircase twisted again after it went past the door he came in through. Maybe he should check it out.

He started walking up the stairs, a little more confidently now. The stairs looked dark and he couldn't see much. Then a loud snap as Marcus's foot went through the rotten wood in the staircase. He gasped, as he felt his foot slide into something wet and slimy and pain pierced his ankle. He looked down, but it was now too dark to see anything. The smell was now a lot stronger he noticed, as he struggled to pull his foot out of the hole in the stairs, but to no avail. He was starting to get rather paranoid now, and he took a deep breath to try and get a hold of himself.

"For fuck's sake, calm down," he whispered.

96

Reaching for his pocket light, Marcus switched it on and looked down. Yep, his foot had gone right through the stair and the wood seemed to have protruded through the skin. After a few attempts of lifting his foot met with fresh pain, he decided he'd have to pull out more of the wood.

A loud snap made him freeze again. There were now louder sounds, getting closer to him and his heart starting beating faster again in his chest.

Quickly, and congratulating himself on bringing the torch, he yanked the wood so he could get his foot out safely. Curiosity had always been there for Marcus, and now he put the torch down to look at where his foot had been. His legs turned to rubber, and gasping in horror, he saw what appeared to be a corpse. The smell was quite horrific, like it had been there for a matter of weeks but its sickly grin was still identifiable on its face. Marcus tried to scream, as he realised his foot had been lodged in a corpse's intestines, but no sound managed to come out of his dry mouth.

Apart from the rapid beating in his own chest, he could hear something else now, too.

It was a heavy sound, like raspy breathing. Shaking, he finally found the courage inside that he needed to look up, and as he did so, he realised the stairs were now almost completely black, bathed in shadow. Looking down at him, were two large dark red eyes, the rest of this horrific sight was still bathed in darkness and he finally managed to scream as the thing came out of the dark, lunged at him and ripped him to shreds in a matter of seconds.

The whole room had been quiet while Beth recounted her story to Xanther. Luke had been her brother, but had been savagely taken away from her by the gang in question. Tears were slowly dripping down her pale cheeks and her body had started to tremble: a vast difference to the bright confidence she had exuded the day before.

Sam sighed, and said, "Where's Marcus? Why didn't he want to come?"

"Ermmm… said something about checking a few things out, told us to give Beth his love though," replied Vincent. Beth smiled.

"Well, I hope he's okay…" said Beth.

"Oh yeah, sure he'll be. You never have to worry about Marcus. He can take care of himself no problem," said Sam, glancing at his watch for a second time.

The group had been talking for an hour and a half, and whatever was going on the night before, Xanther had guessed, was not pleasant. They hadn't gone into much detail, but he knew about the woman who was presumed dead.

"Hey, maybe we should get going now, find out what Marcus's up to," said Sam, in what Xanther thought to be a forced calmness.

Daire seemed to take a measured silence, then said, "Yeah, we'd better check what he's been up to." The group stood up, ready to leave.

"Wait, will you tell me more when you know?" asked Beth apprehensively.

Sam gave her a friendly smile, "Yeah, of course we will. But are you sure you want to know?"

"I'm worried, Sam. Whether I'll want to or not, I have to know. I want to," she replied, her expression so serious he was forced to take it that way.

"Yes, I know. Thanks for having us round, I tell you what we know."

"When we know," added Vincent.

Chapter Eleven

Freya

Freya sat down beside the fire, gently brushing her hair and tugging at the knots. It was 8 pm now, as she watched the flames glowing brightly. She leaned in closer to the heat, reached out to the flames and slowly put her hand through the fire, and back again. Freya looked at her hand, concentrating on something, She didn't quite know what. Then she put out her hand once more, and moved it in and out of the flames, back and forth, back and forth, watching as her hand somehow magically didn't get burned. She wasn't stupid, she knew that playing with fire hurt you, but when it could be controlled…it was pretty.

She missed her brothers; although they showered her with attention and tried to bring her up properly she hated being lied to. She wondered what her parents had been like, how they would have treated her. She knew that was something she'd never find out. Being January, it was still really cold, so she went to get another log for the fire from the shed.

She walked out into the garden, where a cold breeze hit her instantly, blowing her blonde wispy hair onto her face and making her shiver slightly, wrapping her arms around herself as she walked across the garden. The flowers in the garden had grown to be quite wild, the grass was long and weeds tangled around her legs. When she got to the shed, she lifted a large log from the pile, and using all her strength, carried it back to the house. All the time her conscious thoughts of night monsters followed her, getting tangled up in the garden plants and scrambling to get free from time to time. Or at least in her head they did.

"Warm in here," she said, talking to herself. Freya carefully placed the log on top of the others and warmed her hands until they no longer felt numb. Then, she got up and found a candle out of the drawer.

"Something's wrong," she said, matter of factly. Her expression was serious and worriedly she looked out of the window. There was nothing to see, as she listened to the eerie sound of the wind, blowing past the house. The fire crackled on the hearth. She was home alone, not uncommon for children these days. Freya nodded, then took out a match and lit the candle, saying to herself, "Please leave us alone…I don't like you."

Just then, her brothers walked in loudly, talking about the upcoming festival.

"Hey, you've been gone a while," said Freya, then worriedly, "Where's Marcus? Is he okay?"

"Ermm… he had business to catch up on. He'll probably be late. Have you been okay here on your own?" asked Sam, forcing a smile for his little sister. Freya knew he was lying.

"Yeah, I've been watching television. I tried to write a story but I kind of got bored and gave up," she replied happily. She watched her brothers carefully. There were things they weren't telling her, things they didn't want to tell her. She contemplated telling them she knew, but she couldn't possibly know about most things; she was too young.

"Did you see Beth today?" she asked Sam.

"Yeah, we talked for a bit," Sam replied, smiling at the question and the little girl that seemed such an adult these days.

"Who was that guy she was with? Was that her boyfriend?" Freya asked, showing an interest. She'd always liked Beth although at times she seemed almost to be a little bit lost in herself, her thoughts.

"Yeah, I think so, honey. Why?"

"Nothing really, just wondered who he was." She shrugged, getting up once more giving Vincent a concerned look before walking out of the room and running upstairs. Vincent looked back at her, worried. She was definitely acting a little off today.

"Do you think she's okay?" he asked.

"I don't know," Sam sighed, "I hope so. Do you think she knows anything we don't?"

"Doubt it," replied Vincent, deep in thought. Marcus hadn't been seen since that morning. Sam was getting considerably more worried about it, although if these were normal circumstances he wouldn't have to be.

Freya was in her room, and after switching on the light she crept over to the window, opening it a crack. Looking out she felt something out there. She knew what she was feeling; fear. Quietly she whispered the words she knew were true, "Marcus died." Tears slowly trickling down her cheeks, she sat on her bed and contemplated what to do next.

Sam sat with a beer in his hand, watching the others thoughtfully.

"He's probably okay, right? I mean, he's always okay." said Vincent, not convincing himself or any of the others. The fire still burned brightly and the brothers welcomed the warmth after feeling the bitter cold of the town.

"We should never have let him go on his own. I think he might have gone to see what they were doing last night..." Kordian had uttered the words all four of them had been thinking all day. Sam thought it best not to go back there, not yet and so instead of coming with the rest of them to meet with Beth, he

101

had gone there to 'check things out'. Sam thought this was something Marcus would probably do, and dread filled his stomach every time he thought of those terrible noises that woman had made, the sound of the thing that had quelled them…and then silence.

"Sam, maybe we should…" Daire didn't finish his sentence, as he knew what Sam would say. Sam looked at him, then down at himself.

"I think you're right," he sighed, "But if anyone is going down there, it's me."

Vincent looked up sharply, "No! You are not going on your own, we need to stick together." He was not going to let Sam be brave this time, no matter how much of a coward he was.

"I agree with you," said Daire. Kordian looked deep in thought, but nodded in agreement with Vincent and Daire. Just then, a loud scream came from outside. The brothers looked at each other, before standing up and rushing to the door.

Freya was at the top of the stairs, looking pale. "What was that?" she asked.

"We're going to check, you stay here!" exclaimed Vincent. Sam was already out the door and the others were right behind him. Vincent went too, and as soon as he got outside, he got the shock of his life.

Chapter Twelve

Raguals

There were five people gathered outside, two men and three women. Two of the women were standing behind one of the men, who was restraining the third woman. She had been screaming and she looked hysterical and terrified. The second man was across the other side of the street, holding a large stick and trying to defend himself from some kind of large strange creature. Whatever it was, it definitely was not something they had ever seen before.

The four brothers watched as the man took out a lighter and set fire to the branch, waving it at the creature about twice the size of him.

The creature itself was some sort of dark wild beast, only it wasn't quite real – solid looking, and its outline seemed to blend into the air around them. It was raised off the ground and seemed to hover with malevolence. It was startled at the lighted branch and with the arrival of more onlookers and people screaming in shock, it ran off.

Vincent noticed the man had been injured; he had a large cut on his left arm, possibly from the creature's claws. The woman, who had been released, ran across to her husband and the two embraced. Murmurs and exclamations could be heard from all across the street as they realised just what the escapee could mean. Sam and the others ran up to the injured man, to make sure he was okay.

"What in God's name *was* that?" cried the man, looking at the wound on his arm for the first time.

"I don't know," replied Sam, "We've got to get you to a hospital; your arm looks pretty nasty."

"It just came out of nowhere. As I was reaching for the stick it went for me! I thought it would kill me…it felt like it was sucking the soul right out of me," said the wounded man, shivering.

"Yeah, somebody get him to a hospital," said Vincent before turning to Sam and whispering, "I don't know what the hell that was, but let's follow it!" The others agreed, and as the onlookers recovered from the shock of what they had just seen, the four brothers ran after it. Sam had brought his gun and he would use it if he had to.

"Hey, where are you going? Don't leave me here alone!"

Sam turned back, "Freya! You get in the house and stay there, okay? It's not safe outside!"

"No, I want to come with you! Please!"

"Get inside. We won't be long," called Vincent, before following his brothers in the direction the creature ran.

They ran through the darkness, towards the town. The stars shone brightly down on them and the moon was full. It was mostly silent, as the brothers decided what route the creature had taken. Then suddenly there were screams ahead, people were running down from the entrance to Broad Street.

Sam took one look at the frightened people and said to the others, "Problem solved, let's go that way."

As the four proceeded, they heard yet more evidence of disruption up ahead. Vincent's legs felt like jelly, but he somehow managed to keep up with his brothers. A girl he knew, Lydia, was running the other way.

"Vincent! Are you crazy? Don't tell me you are chasing after that thing!" Lydia cried, grabbing hold of his arm.

"Lydia, go where it's safe! I'll be fine; I'm going to find out what that thing is."

Lydia sighed, looked into his eyes and said, "Be careful, I think it's heading towards town." Vincent nodded, then ran up to Sam, who had stopped to fully load his gun. Sam saw Vincent and gave him a look of reassurance.

"Come on, we have to bring it down before it does any more harm."

"Well, it seems to be quite confused. Maybe it's not that dangerous," Kordian replied, looking every bit the animal lover he secretly was.

"Not dangerous! Did you see that guy's arm? I think we need to stop it, and fast!" Daire argued, brandishing his knife.

"I bet it has something to do with Neil. This is what he was holding last night, the noises from the warehouse." Sam said, angrily, "Come on, it'll be in town by now!" Sam cried. The four continued down the street and into Main Street, where they could see many people panicking. There was more of a crowd in the square, and Sam rushed forward, only to be held back by Vincent.

"What are you doing Vince?"

"Be careful! You don't know what that thing can do!"

"Okay, okay! We need to stop it, before it does any more damage so let go of me!" Vincent let go and he rushed forward, followed by Daire, then Kordian. Vincent was just about to follow, when he heard Beth shout, "Vincent, over here!" He turned around and saw her standing there, beside Xanther, who seemed like a good guy, Vincent thought.

"Hey! You guys stand back. That thing's dangerous! Leave it to us!" he called. There were now a number of horrified people looking on; too scared to even run they all stood watching Sam. Sam was now aiming his gun at the creature, which was now focused on two young girls. It had backed them into a corner and looked like it was about to strike. Sam fired his gun, and the creature visibly recoiled. It turned to face Sam, and he fired at it again, this time in its side. The creature squealed, making Beth grimace at the sound of its inhuman pain. Sam and the others watched as it made a movement to touch its wound, then, surprisingly fast it ran past the girls and soon it was out of sight. One of the young girls then fainted, and their mother ran to them screaming, joined by a few others.

Just then another beast roared through the area, knocking a man to the ground and charging through one of the houses; screams grew through the town and the group looked at each other in fear, and at the utter pandemonium around them.

Soon they were joined by other town folk, attracted by the small crowd that had gathered, thinking it must be safe.

Xanther looked around at the devastation the thing had caused. The town was a mess. He turned to face Vincent and asked, "What the hell were those things? Where did they come from?"

Vincent shrugged, "I don't know. We've been chasing one of them from the other side of town. No idea what they are." Sam walked towards them, followed by Daire. Kordian surveyed the damage around the square as people asked him what had just gone on.

"It's dangerous here, we've got to get out of town! I don't know what is going on but it's far from safe."

"Hey, what was that? What's going on?"

"Freya! What are you doing here? I told you to stay put!" Sam shouted and then put his hand up to his head, angry with himself for shouting. She was scared. He could see that.

"I'm sorry… I wanted to know what was happening. I was worried."

"So, what do we do now?" asked Beth. She looked so pale standing there, Xanther put his arms around her and she shivered.

"We have to leave here. I say we should go and get some supplies and leave for the forest, until we know what the hell we're dealing with," replied Sam.

"The forest? Are you sure?" Beth looked at Sam with worried eyes.

"Yes, I don't think it's safe for any of us here. I've suspected so for a long time, I'll tell you all about it when we get there." He was beginning to relax slightly, and most of the people from town had left the streets, probably to hide in their homes, possibly to flee the town like they were. Not that there were many people in the town to worry about, and the others could not be messed with.

The group headed back to the Cullen house, to stock up before departing for the outskirts. Luckily they did not come into contact with the creatures again, and they walked through the darkness to safety. Beth needed to rest, but she was thankful that she and Xanther had run into Sam. They would need his help, and his brothers. Freya stayed quiet all the way back.

The group had assembled calmly in the living room of the Cullens house. It was now about 8:30 pm and Sam had just finished packing enough food and just about everything else they were going to need. Beth looked troubled, and huddled close to Xanther on the sofa. He stroked her hair, as he conversed with Vincent about what was going on.

"I have a bad feeling about all this...I mean, where could those things have come from? Is there more?" Xanther said.

Vincent sighed, "I don't know. Whatever it was, I wouldn't like to run into one of those on my own. Did you see its eyes? They were bright red."

Beth shivered again. "Do you really think leaving town is necessary?"

"Yes, we don't have many other options. Best thing to do is go by foot, into the outskirts. There are friendly people there. We just need to find them and they will protect us until we know what to do."

"Do you have friends that live there?" asked Beth, worried but intrigued at the idea of the forest.

"Yeah, kind of. We'll be safe for a while. The settlers are kind, warm people, and we need to warn them. "

She looked relieved at that. "Okay, then we can maybe find some answers," she smiled. "Xanther, why are you so quiet?"

"Don't know. I'm still in shock I guess. That thing was big, and I was just wondering where it came from...?"

Just then the others entered the room. Sam looked around at them. "Everything okay?"

"Yeah, we're all fine," replied Xanther.

"Right, time to go," said Sam. Everyone got up, fully prepared for whatever they had front of them. Kordian opened the front door, and stepped out first into the cold night air. Looking around, he could see nothing threatening, and motioned for the others to follow. There was a group of people ahead, and overhearing them Xanther knew they were leaving town too.

"Hey, maybe you should come with us, it's not safe on your own," Sam told them. They kept on walking, until they got into a car, obviously intending to drive to the nearest place they thought was safe.

"Hey, wait!" Vincent shouted. They did not listen and headed for the town centre, and then, who knew where. Xanther doubted whether they'd make it to wherever they were going, as the roads were probably blocked up by this time, by everyone else with the same idea. Or the police...or quarantine for that matter. Xanther didn't believe it could have gone that far yet, but he didn't know much at that moment in time. He didn't trust the authorities in the slightest, since the town had been left to recede by itself.

The seven of them had wrapped up warmly and were now heading out into the streets again. Xanther felt they were somewhat vulnerable, as it was dark, and extremely quiet now. Luckily Sam and the others lived on the outside of town anyway, so they didn't have to walk like this for long.

Xanther trusted Sam's judgement. He wondered what kind of people were actually in the forest, and why they were there. He found it strange that people would live there. He'd never been in it himself but imagined it a dark and forbidding place. Somewhere that, when you were a child, you'd think the monsters dwelled there, when actually they dwelled in the dark scary pit of your own mind. His monster used to live there, turning his life into some sort of prison until Beth came along and led it softly away. Beth was like that. He was grateful for her.

When they had reached the edge of the town, where the concrete ended and the trees began, Beth started to look very worried, constantly making sure the amulet never left her neck in the darkness. It glowed up at her.

"Are you sure there is anyone in there? Are you sure it's safe?" asked Beth, contemplating entering the large forest that lay ahead of her.

"Yes, it's safe. The settlers may have moved on, but I doubt it. The forest is something of a second home to them. It holds a special meaning. They always return there and besides, they should be warned. I know my way around so don't worry," replied Sam. He looked round at the rest of the group, who all seemed just about ready to go. Daire and Kordian looked at Sam concernedly, not sure he was ready to face the settlement once again.

A lot had happened there long ago that had changed his life forever. It had been a difficult coping process but he got through it. The only thing was, he hadn't been back there since.

"I'm not sure I want to go," Daire said, catching the attention of Sam.

"We've got no choice," Sam replied, looking convinced that their only option was to run.

"What about all the people in the underground, will they be safe down there?"

"We should be protecting them," he replied, firmly.

"We'll find a way to protect them, Daire. I don't think those things will be able to get to them underground. They'll be safe. They'll seal the gates if they have to."

Beth was huddled up close to Xanther, who was looking at the forest with an amused expression on his face. Freya was holding on tightly to Daire's leg, and he lifted her up onto his shoulders. Vincent was sitting on a nearby rock, looking at the ground. Kordian was ready to go, and stood boldly with his rucksack, the look of experienced traveller on his face. Sam himself had a large haversack on his back, and both of them looked prepared. Daire had a smaller bag and between them they carried everything they should need. Vincent had a tent while Xanther carried the rest of the supplies.

He noticed Beth's eyes, shining in the dark and he squeezed her hand firmly.

"Everyone got everything? Right, let's go." Sam announced. Vincent got up, and they proceeded into the dark forest towards whatever awaited them in the shadows.

Chapter Thirteen

Luann

It was dusty and dark outside that night and the atmosphere was dry when she arrived at this empty, cold town. She wasn't prepared; tears were still drying on her eyes, marked by mascara. The moon shone down on her, partially obscured by clouds. Her heart filled with emotion that she kept far down inside. Her thoughts were bitter, an escape from responsibility and her selfishness. She felt like nothing; like everything, her wants and needs completely condensed into this one feeling. Overpowered with need she was hungry for salvation or sin. She walked alongside the cornfield, feeling the cool air on her skin.

It was already late when she entered the bar. Smoke filled her lungs and she made an attempt to rectify her mussed hair in the ladies' room filled with sprays and the smell of perfume to choke on. Her dark blue eyes shone back at her in the mirror. She wiped them clean. Her red top shined under the overhead lights. Whispering behind her, she had no time for the opinions of others. Pushing through the double doors she entered the bar and ordered a Grand Marnier. It was then the music started to play in this quiet town.

It filled the bar, the sweet chords striking at her heart in an almost painful way she never wanted to stop. She sat there for a moment, transfixed before the singer's voice reached her ears. It was then she turned to watch the singer with a mass of hair and the unusual, tall figure beside him. Luann had never heard such beauty, completely transfixed to where this person was taking her. The voice filled her ears but seemed to blend into the music like it was secondary. It overtook her completely.

The bar filled with people, the murmuring of everyday life hummed in the background. Smoke circled around her and she sat nursing her drink, not paying attention to the other men watching her.

The player watched her, his eyes piercing hers. She sat, suddenly so conscious of herself not caring, to prove to herself she wasn't the person they thought she was, her child left behind waiting for her.

The music settled down, began to slow and quieten and the lights already dim were starting to come softly back up. She summoned the nerve to look at him again. Putting down the guitar, his soulful eyes preoccupied, he represented a saviour.

Sipping the sweet drink, she cast her gaze at him like a spell. His head turned sharply and he was looking at her again, like she was the only person in the room. She knew then she wanted him, but she didn't know exactly what she wanted. To be a goddess, to be in the spotlight for just one night? Disregarding the old feelings she became Luann again, the girl that knew what she wanted and how to play.

He approached her as the old jukebox began to play some old country song. Pretending at first not to notice, she then looked up through blonde thick locks of hair and smiled. Sitting across from her, this creature looked wise and yet young, graceful yet so perfectly manly; his eyes a deep blue, his skin a soft pale colour.

"Hi, I'm Billy," he spoke to her, his voice audible like a soft velvet over the sounds of the bar; sitting so relaxed in front of her, this creature that looked like a man but played like an angel.

"I'm Luann," spoke the trailer trash girl. She feigned calm as she played with the gold rings on her fingers, her eyes looking down then up through thick mascara. The lipstick had worn off long ago, and her vulnerability showed through her girlish face. Billy smiled kindly at her.

"You sounded great tonight," she told him.

"Oh, thank you," he spoke, looking down at his hands. His voice was smooth but sweet like caramel. She felt herself being so helplessly fascinated. His surreal air did not fade when they started to speak more; as she had expected it to. Billy asked her where she was from. Luann found herself concealing her rings from this being. Smiling, she moved her hair back from her face and their hands touched. The music played on in the background, seducing her senses and making the smoky bar seem even more dreamlike. They talked about everything but what was bothering her, which was silently apparent to Billy; the trouble on her face. Their thighs brushed lightly, and then stayed that way.

A couple started arguing beside them, breaking the passing of hours and bringing her out of the dream. It was almost 1am and she became very aware of where she was. Billy's hand was touching hers; it felt cool but not unpleasant. A sudden feeling of time running out became obvious to her, and she remembered once again why she was here in the first place. Her hurt became drawn on her face; her hand went once more to her hair and pushed it back from her face, preoccupied now with her inner self. It was then she made the decision.

"Do you want to go somewhere with me?" she asked, her eyes meeting up with Billy as she looked at him. He looked back questioning, a quizzical smile on his face and he silently agreed.

The sudden cold hit her as they got outside, the dark of the night making Billy look almost translucent, apparitional. Billy;

her protector, her guide, her ruin. She wanted him to be the latter but her heart cried out to be helped. She led him by the hand and stopped herself from feeling sad once more. Turning to him, she pulled him towards her, towards the cornfield. He obliged, moving close to her. He gently touched her shoulders and leaned in, ever so softly to kiss her. That was all she needed. Pulling him into the field, their bodies together, legs clumsy they kissed and her memories flooded into her mind. What they were doing now, what she had felt when she met him and then all the bad things, the fight, the tears, the shouting… and then he was on top of her. Her clothes were being removed and she lost herself in him. She thought back to the happiness she had shared, the joy. She thought of what she had left behind; her obligation. His touch on her body overtook the thoughts once more in this race against herself; she wondered again deeply why she was doing this.

Tears were building in her eyes. She felt his tongue and remembered that day when she thought the whole world was going to end, but didn't. The day when she came into Luann's life, and filled her world with light; Mary. Her child; her beautiful little girl she'd left behind.

Entombing herself in his embrace, she felt that warmth and overcame her fears, her worries and she realised it wasn't so bad. Billy was looking at her smile and smiled back, confused slightly. He leaned away from her, and she wiped away the tears childishly from her cheeks. She stood, and began to look through the rows of corn as if searching for something; perhaps herself.

"It's times like these you feel so small…"

"I hope you found what you were looking for," Billy replied from behind her now, touching her shoulder with his lip. She felt his breath against her.

It was when she turned around, she noticed Billy was gone. Looking around, startled she realised she was completely alone and blinking, shaking slightly, she began to make her way back towards the road; towards home.

He let her go, even though her soul was calling out to be taken and his hunger yearned for her, to put her out of her misery, to smell her blood. But soon his thirst would be quenched for real.

Chapter Fourteen

The Forest

The seven figures had walked for almost four hours and it was safe to say they were all fairly tired. It was long past Freya's bedtime, and she was beginning to fall asleep on Daire's shoulders.

"You're hardly a featherweight any more you know: How long do you think I'll be able to carry you all this way?" Daire replied to her jokingly, when again she complained of her tiredness. She giggled half-heartedly. They were now far into the forest, the darkness surrounding them as the trees covered most of the moonlight. Beth wanted to see the stars again. She was feeling a bit claustrophobic, although she kept telling herself there was no need for that. Xanther held on to her tight, because every time she heard a noise of some sort, she jumped slightly. He could tell that she was nervous.

"Right," Sam sighed, "I think we should all get some rest, so let's just stop here for the night. We're safe from whatever it was we saw tonight. I think we all need to crash."

"Okay, let's make a fire," said Vincent, and they all chipped in to help with the firewood, although no one wandered far that night. Soon there was a bright fire, and they all huddled round it.

They talked for a while, none of them really wanting to sleep now the time had actually come. Soon they noticed that Freya was sleeping soundly, so Sam started to set up a tent for her. Vincent had been mostly quiet all night, and now he sat beside Daire.

"Do you think Marcus is okay?" he asked, quietly.

Daire looked at him closely, not knowing how to answer. "Well, it's been in the back of my mind all night, but I don't know Vince... let's just hope he is."

"Do you think those things...?" Vincent put his head in his hands, unable to finish his sentence. Daire just looked away.

"Hey, we need more firewood," Kordian announced, as he poked the last of the flickering flames, trying to make them last.

"I'll go," Vincent said. He got up and was gone before anyone else could stop him.

"Hey, is he all right?" asked Sam, returning from making up the first tent.

"He's worried about Marcus. Just let him be alone for a few minutes and he'll be back."

"We're all worried about Marcus...Yeah, I guess he needs some space, we all do some times."

"Freya," he whispered to the sleeping girl, "Time to go to bed. Come on..."

"No, let her sleep," said Beth, "Wait, I'll carry her through." She got up, and went over to pick up the sleeping Freya.

"She looks like a little angel," whispered Beth as she picked her up. Xanther watched as she took Freya into the tent to tuck her in.

Beth laid Freya on the made-up bed, and as she was tucking her in, her eyes opened sleepily. Beth smiled at her, and Freya smiled back.

"Goodnight," Freya whispered.

"Goodnight, Sweetie," Beth whispered to her. She kissed her on the forehead, then stepped out of the tent, making sure it was closed. She walked back to the dying flames of the fire, and sat down beside Xanther who kissed her lightly on the lips. They huddled up together, and they waited for Vincent to return with the firewood.

As Sam sat at the camp fire, his mind filled with memories of the place he was about to return to. It had been long ago since he visited Fahra Point. It hurt to think of her name let alone go back there.

The last time he had been to the settlement was in fact to collect his child; the child they bore together to be a symbol of their everlasting love.

Fahra had been young when they'd found out she was pregnant. A settler she had been taken in by the colony when she was still a child.

They had fallen in love while Sam stayed at the camp on his travels. He had made himself very welcome there.

He remembered her long red hair as she washed it in the river, the bump that he knew was their baby growing inside of her. Her eyes had been a beautiful green and she had been so happy and vibrant. With her pregnancy she seemed to glow.

He would have stayed at that settlement forever, just to be with her and their child.

If it were a boy, he would have called him Ali. Sam used to spend nights lying awake in bed, his beautiful girl sleeping next to him, thinking about what the baby would look like. He would have preferred if it had looked like her instead of him, as he never thought of himself as that attractive.

Sometimes Fahra would wake up and ask him what he was thinking, although deep down he was convinced she knew how happy she and the baby had made him.

When the baby started to kick, everything suddenly seemed so real to Sam and it had never made him happier. He knew from then on that nothing could change the process of their lives; it was up to them to make a home.

He never questioned how she had felt about the pregnancy; she seemed to be so happy as she talked to the lump in her stomach about things like growing up and 'daddy' and life in general. She was young, only seventeen but there had never been a more wanted baby.

"So Sam," she would say, "How do you want this baby to grow up?"

He had laughed, "Well, I don't know…in a nurturing environment I suppose, somewhere peaceful like this."

She shook her head, replying, "No, no, no… I want this baby to grow up in the city with friends and colours and sounds. You know, plenty of distractions and variety, like how you grew up." She sounded so sure of herself when she had told him that and it had made him smile, knowing she wanted the baby to grow up like he had.

Looking back, he knew he was in love with her and wanted to protect her with all his heart but for some reason, as he sat there in the forest waiting for Vincent, the love that he once felt had gone from his heart.

He couldn't even remember the feeling anymore, like his heart had turned to stone.

The night that Fahra gave birth had been a dramatic one; she screamed in pain and her labour seemed to go on for hours. But finally the end result produced a beautiful baby girl that he instantly fell in love with.

Fahra had been exhausted that first night, too tired to hold the baby for more than five minutes before she fell asleep.

He held and fed that little girl on that night until early morning when one of the female settlers took over and he could get some rest.

119

He entered the tent where Fahra lay and got in next to her, whispering, "She's so beautiful, darling. You did such a good job."

"I love you, Sam," she whispered to him, "You mean so much to me. Promise to look after her." At the time he hadn't really understood what she had meant.

Fahra smiled as she drifted off to sleep, looking content and squeezing his hand in hers. She didn't seem as bright as usual, but considering what she'd gone through he didn't think much of it as he watched her sleeping silently.

The next few days had been some of the happiest of his life as he watched Fahra playing with the baby, clothing her and feeding her. He had his turn too, holding her tiny hands in his and marvelling at how delicate she was.

One week later, Fahra had seemed much quieter than usual. Sam walked in on her as she brushed her long red hair down her back, shining beautifully in the light from the window. Her face was calm but unsmiling, the baby asleep in the cot next to her.

He remembered thinking that something was wrong, but at the time, he didn't risk asking her what. He regretted that later.

The settlers had given them their own small cabin. They recognised that the young family should be given space and Sam was very thankful for their kindness.

It was the middle of the night when he woke up to the sound of the baby crying.

He muttered, "Shhh, it's all right," as he began to pull himself out of bed, looking around for Fahra.

A strange feeling entered his stomach when he realised she was not in the cabin. It was dark and silent outside, around 4:20 am and right away he knew, somehow that she was not in the woods any more.

Cradling the baby in his arms he walked out into the settlement, no shoes on his feet and called her name. No answer came as he shouted for her again and again.

Some of the settlers had joined him to find out what had happened, and together they searched for her high and low. Nothing.

That morning around four hours later they found her clothes by the lake, with no explanation and no trace of a footprint.

Sam had searched that lake, diving in again and again only to surface for air to breathe. They found nothing. He had cried for days, refusing to look at the little girl that Fahra had brought into the world. The women settlers fed and bathed her until he could take responsibility of the child.

Eventually they gave up looking for her and after a while, Sam had returned to Middletown with a newborn baby that he swore with his life to look after, love and protect. Only he hadn't been ready to take on such a responsibility on his own.

Now as he sat contemplating the settlement, the pain he felt that day, he dreaded returning to Fahra Point.

Vincent trudged through the forest, picking up branches here and there. Not that he could see that well since it was so dark. He had been thinking to himself for a while now and had probably walked further from the camp than he had intended to. He thought about Marcus, and where he could be at that moment. Had he encountered the beasts they had met in town? Or was he still unaware that anything was wrong? He could be back at the house right now and wondering where they were.

Vincent wasn't really looking where he was going, as he was watching his feet and gathering bits of wood. He had quite a big bundle by now and was about to head back for camp, if he could find it. Just then he looked up, and saw some light through the bushes. He stopped and listened intently. And music, he could hear music! He crept forward a little, and soon enough he saw what looked like a large fire burning, and people, quite a few of them. He watched them. They all seemed to be wearing strange clothes. Maybe these were the settler group his brother had been talking about. A few of them were gathered around the fire, and he could see a few lumps behind them, covered in blankets. There were a couple of women sitting there, talking and eating what looked like bread.

Vincent stepped a little closer when a branch snapped under his foot, causing one of the women to look straight at him. Registering her surprise, she stood up, and then took a step towards him. Vincent stepped forward also, and the music soon stopped as everyone turned to look at him. She quickly turned around and a shrieking noise filled the camp that hurt Vincent's ears.

Then, just like that, the fire disappeared. Everything seemed to die out, the noise and the light, and through the black there was movement. Something large brushed right past him made him jump and the feeling of fear he had felt earlier took complete control of his nerves. He uttered a small sound before running, stumbling as far as he could to get away from whatever the noise was coming from. The noise itself was indescribable and sent shivers all down his body. It was the noise of something *alive*, something that seemed both frightening and terribly unnatural.

The people he had glimpsed were just a mere thought now, and hardly an important one. He had to get away. The feeling was so intense whatever it was. He hated that thing, hated the noise. He put his hands over his ears, his face twisted into a grimace and he turned away. He started to run.

The noise of his own heart, the crushing of branches under his feet mixed together with the sounds of the bushes and trees he brushed past in his panic, drowned out most of the other noise. He ran; the trees scraping his arms and ripping his shirt, his pile of firewood long forgotten about, discarded somewhere on the ground. Until bit by bit, he realised he could not hear anything else. He stopped, his breathing rugged and heavy. His heart felt like it was almost in his throat.

He stood, supported by a tree, shaking and shivering all over. He felt cold, and looking around, he didn't know where he was. Vincent took a deep breath, trying to think.

"Shit," he sighed. Again, the feeling almost flooded his mind and he realised he had to find the others, warn them. Dazedly, he stumbled around, leaning on trees for support, his grazed legs shaking. His heart beat fast in his chest and the feeling of panic started to set in. What a fool he had been to go so far anyway. And who were those people?

He started to walk faster, looking for the light of the fire if it was still lit, and all the time it was rising inside him.

Just when he felt he was about to scream, he saw the light through the trees. It was his brothers sitting there, and Beth. His beating heart skipped slightly and using all his strength he ran through the trees, catching everyone's attention all at once. Beth gasped and her face grew white as he stood in front of her. His shirt was ripped badly and there were scratches down his arms. A large red cut was on his left cheek. Beth spoke first.

"W-what happened?" she stuttered, slowly getting up. Her nerves were already on full alert and she still felt the adrenalin rush from earlier. Sam had turned from fixing up a tent and the others had looked up from where they were sitting. Their faces reminded Vincent of chalk, he thought crazily. He laughed slightly. The sound hardly uttered at all.

"Vin, are you all right? What happened? Tell us," Sam spoke softly, barely able to contain his voice from getting louder.

"I… I don't know exactly. I went on a walk and there were these people at a camp fire. There was a few of them then the light just went out and… and something was chasing me and I ran like hell and we'd better get out of here!"

"What was it Vincent?" asked Beth, steadily, her eyes wide.

"Whatever it was, it was unnatural. That sound…" His legs were shaking so badly he slowly leaned his weight against one of the trees again.

"We have to pack up and put out the fire. It could be drawn to us," replied Sam, "Who were those people? Was it the settlers?"

"I only saw them for a few moments. They saw me then I heard this… this *thing* and the light went out and I heard whatever it was and a lot of rustling. It scared the hell out of me and all I could think about was to get away. Don't know how long I ran for. I thought I was lost."

Beth came to him first and trying to support him with her weight she helped him sit. She kneeled down in front of him, and his hand instinctively grasped hers. She looked into his eyes, and he saw hers were frightened. The feeling of panic had not yet died away and he could hear the others asking him questions. Beth spoke.

"Vincent, is there something behind us? Is it still coming?"

Shaking his head hopelessly he replied, "God, I don't know. It could be." He paused slightly, "Beth, I just ran." Beth looked behind him, into the blackness. She could make out the shapes of trees until they faded away into black. There was something in his voice, something that made her believe it was in there somewhere.

"We have to get out," said Xanther, taking hold of her hand. He had heard everything.

"Everyone, pack your stuff. We need to try and find my friends, the settlers tonight. They could be in danger," Sam said, kneeling down and loosening the tent pegs. He thought it was probably the same people that Vincent had seen; they often went out to hunt and relaxed at night, sometimes played music. That was when he had been there. The forest looked dark and uninviting to him now, and he suddenly felt slightly lost. He

124

noticed his hands were also shaking slightly as he felt for his rucksack, and he felt himself wish for the daylight to come.

Kordian watched his brother's shaking hands, and reached out for them, before helping to pack. He smiled, but the smile could not stay on his face.

Everyone slowly, calmly started to get ready to go, silently so that nothing was disturbed.

Freya awoke silently and they started through the woods, heading north-west, opposite from where Vincent had come. Most of the time they stayed quiet with a few disconcerted glances behind them, as not to worry Freya. The young girl only looked confused and sleepy.

A few times, a branch would snap or a creature would rustle behind them. They heard nothing more or less.

After a while, Sam took Freya in his arms.

"If you're not careful you'll collapse, hon," he whispered to her.

Beth glanced over at Xanther, who was shivering slightly. He looked up and smiled at her. They were holding hands, walking near the front. Beth felt like they were lost. It was so dark, and she felt so odd about what had happened in town. It was very quiet in the woods, stunningly quiet. She squeezed Xanther's hand.

Suddenly Sam stopped, motioned them to be still. The others looked at him anxiously, and then Xanther thought he heard a noise in the distance. It was too far away to tell exactly what it was, but it sounded like it was something big by all the rustling and disturbance of the trees. A louder splitting sound echoed through the trees, and something else as well. Beth glanced over at Freya, who was fast asleep in Sam's arms. His face was calm, and she kept listening.

"Do you think it's…" Vincent started.

"Shhh! Listen!" whispered Daire.

Whatever it was, it was too far off to tell where it was or if it was coming closer. Daire thought he didn't want to stick around to find out. He moved forward, and in almost a run they all followed.

Beth was pulled forward by Xanther, and it gave her a jolt of fear inside. She couldn't really see in front of her, and the movement of the others beside her drowned out the already quiet noise of whatever was behind them. Xanther was right next to her, slightly ahead and she could see the black of his hair. He was holding her hand tightly and she was grateful.

The brothers were behind them, Vincent near the back. He didn't feel much of the fear he had felt earlier. What he felt was more of shock.

"Are we going to find them, Sam? Do you know if we're going the right way?"

Sam shook his head, and said, "I'm not sure any more. It's all a bit different in the dark. They might have moved to different parts." He was gently clutching Freya tight to his chest as he spoke. His voice sounded less certain than before.

"I hope we find them before it finds us," replied Daire. Kordian was silent beside him, the sound of his breathing steady. Daire only wished he could see.

Neil was pacing back and forward, his face a mixture of fury and fear. They had gathered round in the alleyway, all four of them. Raoul watched him intensely, disbelieving every word.

"It's escaped and they're fucking everywhere!" Neil shouted. He was shaking all over; his throat was catching and his eyes darted round nervously. Raoul got up in rage.

"What the hell are we supposed to do in this situation? We're terrorists not beast catchers!" His arms flew up over his head. "Did he tell us what to do?"

Weak, Neil sat on the wall. Timmon fidgeted beside him, fear pounding into his heart.

"We'll have to get out of here…" said Neil. The strength in him from just a minute ago had vanished.

"Get out! Yeah like hell we have to get out!" Raoul replied. He began a search for his car keys but then decided he'd left them at the flat.

"We have to get out fast or we're not getting out at all," said Neil, calmly now. "The roads are going to be completely blocked off to keep them from leaving, just like he said they would. I've no idea what those things can do." Raoul groaned in despair. The others watched in silence, fear on every face. Vesra's eyes rested on Timmon as he spoke up.

"What should we do Neil?"

"We need to get to the other side of town. We'll need protection; you and Raoul get the car and take it to Kans street. We'll meet you there and while you're doing that we'll get some money and the weapons. Take this." He handed Timmon a small bag. Timmon quickly stuffed it into his pocket and followed Raoul out into the town, prepared for the destruction that they'd unwittingly caused.

"Why did we do this?" Timmon moaned to himself, continuing, "No amount of money is worth this. Look at the fucking place!" The town was full of panic and gun shots. It was hard to believe that the festival would go ahead as planned, but the Wolf had assured them things would continue no matter what the threat.

He would be there soon, his menacing voice and soulless eyes staring into him; Timmon knew their time was almost up.

It wasn't long until they found the camp built up by the settlers. The unlikely group slowed down to almost a halt as they approached the crackling fire and the murmuring of voices in the camp.

Through the trees, they could see the white canvas tents and few wagons set up next to the fire burning brightly. A few settlers were walking around the site, a couple warming their hands by the fire.

One of them turned to the odd-looking group, and Sam stepped forward first.

"Ermmm… hello. It's Sam. I used to stay here. We came here from town," Sam said.

"Sam, what are you doing here, from town on your own?" asked the man, dressed in rough pale fabrics.

"We've been trying to find you for hours, we set up camp nearby. We think you might be in danger, we have news and we also seek refuge here."

"Refuge! Refuge from what?" asked another man, who had emerged from one of the wooden wagons.

They crowded round the fire, grateful for its warmth as Sam explained to one of the settlers what had been happening in Middletown.

Halfway through, they were joined by an older man with kind eyes and a soft expression. Sam instantly recognised him as Jared.

Jared was a tall man who looked about fifty-something. He had dark-grey hair, long in a kind of pleat going down his back. There was a thin band around his head, and he wore a robe of white with a black vest underneath. Over his robe was a long, loose waistcoat of green. He was also wearing one long gold earring, and he had black sandals on his feet. In his smile Sam could see one gold tooth. Sam had seen him before, although they had not been properly introduced.

"Hello, I'm Sam and these are my brothers. Nice to meet you," Sam said as he shook the hand of one of the settlers.

"Nice to meet you too, I'm Jared," the man replied. "Tell me, what are you doing here so late and why do you seek us?"

"We did not think we would find you tonight, so we set up camp not far away from here," replied Sam. "This is Vincent who you met before, Daire, and Kordian. We are here to seek safety, for the time being and also to warn you."

"Warn us? Please elaborate, but first, sit down and make yourselves comfortable." Jared gestured to the fire. "It's chilly tonight. Would you like a drink of our home broth?" Sam and the others looked around the fireplace. Other men and women sat there, looking friendly and talkative to each other. A man smiled up at them and moved over to make room.

"Yes please. We'd love that. Thank you very much for your kindness."

"Yeah, thanks," said Vincent, amazed at the tiny civilisation going on around him, in the middle of a forest.

"So, please tell us, what is troubled you so much you have fled the town?"

"Well, it's tough to know where to start…"

"There's some kind of… creatures, just attacking people. We managed to chase one away, but we don't know how many there are or where they came from. We don't feel it's safe there. I thought we should warn you in case they find their way here," Vincent explained.

"Oh… beasts, in town? Well, it's good you told us. We best be on guard," Jared sounded worried, and also concerned. "What did these creatures look like, exactly?"

"Bigger than a human, strong looking and… very agile but not quite there," replied Daire as he sipped his broth. Sam contemplated how best to describe it more, but couldn't. Just then, an old friend Sam recognised walked towards them. It was Brent, someone he had known a few years ago, the first time he had met the settlers. He had stayed at their camp in Oka'ha for a few months once, while travelling.

"Sam! What brings you here my friend?" Brent said. He hadn't changed at all. Today he wore light brown trousers, a black torn shirt and a white sash belt. On his feet he wore nothing, and his red hair was tied up with just a tiny pony tail in the back. He had his head shaved at either side, just like always. The settlers were a very laid back group, and did not care much for expensive clothes or anything else materialistic. In fact, they kind of had their own style, and Sam loved that about them. Vincent on the other hand, was eyeing up all the weird clothes these people were wearing and watching them with a kind of fascination that was profoundly childlike.

"Brent! I didn't think I'd see you here. How long's it been, man? Sadly, what brings me here is not good news," replied Sam.

"Oh, well please tell me all about it," Brent said, "I'd be very interested to hear."

"Serious matters," explained Sam.

"Hey, we've got a very sleepy little girl here," Xanther told them.

"Yes, I don't think she can keep her eyes open much longer," said Beth.

Jared got to his feet and introduced himself to Xanther and Beth, before saying, "Right, let's get this child to bed. I'm sure we've got plenty space for all of you, at a squeeze."

"Oh, well thank you, Jared," said Beth, trying to stifle a yawn. "I think I'll go have a sleep too, if that's all right with everyone?"

"Yes, of course it is," replied Jared, "I'll show you both to where you will be sleeping."

"Okay, goodnight, everyone." Beth waved to them all. She kissed Xanther, and then followed Jared who was finding them somewhere to stay.

Beth was shown somewhere for her and Freya to sleep for the night, and had no problems with getting Freya to sleep. It was warm inside the cabin, and Beth wrapped her up with plenty of blankets.

She left her belongings beside the sleeping child and deciding she could not sleep right away, rejoined the rest of the group, who had by now woken most of the other settlers. They crowded round with worried expressions as Sam described the beasts which had earlier attacked the town.

Jared listened with a steady gaze on Sam, sometimes looking to the others who agreed with Sam's story. After a while he motioned for them to stop.

"Sam, I am glad you have come here after what has happened. We are all very grateful for your warning," he spoke softly, as most of the others had gone back to bed.

He continued, "But for now we are safe, and you should rest now while you still have the chance. Today, we will decide what actions to take."

"I'll rest, but I don't think sleep will come easy to any of us tonight," Xanther said, holding Beth's hand.

Some of the men had volunteered to stand guard for the rest of the early hours, while the group got some rest in their beds. Eventually they all made their way to sleep as the night sounds echoed around them.

Chapter Fifteen

Secrets and Guilt

When Beth awoke, she could see it was still dark as night. Her dreams had been haunted and confused. She could hear the sound of crickets and…she realised she had woken to the sound of Xanther's voice not too far away.

Looking beside her, she could see that Freya was still sound asleep, her golden hair trailing over her pillow. Carefully and quietly she got out of bed and tiptoed outside, being sure not to wake up the sleeping angel. The stars shone brightly up in the sky, as Xanther sat talking to Jared. The night had progressed far, but Xanther felt too awake to sleep that night; perhaps old habits do die hard.

Jared sat by the fire, nursing the flames and wrapped up warmly in a shawl. He looked like a wise man. Xanther was admiring the view of the sky, as he contemplated the words that Jared spoke, softly but seriously.

"Well, all that happened a long time ago," Jared continued, "Sam could tell you all about it. She was a beautiful girl, always seemed to be in touch with nature. He knew her very well." Jared was discussing the disappearance of Fahra, one of the settlers. Fahra had disappeared in these very woods almost ten years ago, and that was the reason the colony had moved on.

"So, after a while you came back?"

"Yes, four years ago. Although we still mourn the loss of Fahra, we could never find somewhere like this anywhere in Orenia. We have travelled for a while, but this is the place we came back to, as it has so many memories and good times for us. We named the settlement Fahra Point."

"Oh, look who has joined us," Jared said, looking past Xanther and up at Beth, who stood sleepily rubbing her eyes. Xanther turned and smiled at Beth, who in turn smiled back, tugging her fingers through her tangled hair, trying to fix it.

"I woke up and I heard you talking... can I join in?"

"Yes, certainly you can. But I must leave you now. My old bones grow stiff. I bid you goodnight."

"Oh, well goodnight, sleep well," Xanther told him.

"Yes, goodnight, Jared," added Beth, watching sleepily as Jared stood up slowly and made his way into one of the trailers giving them one last look. Beth sat down beside Xanther at the fireside, and he held her close to him.

"So, what were you two talking about?" she had asked after she kissed him.

"I was interested in how these people came to live here, and why they prefer somewhere like this to living in a technology-orientated civilisation," Xanther replied. He kissed her on the cheek and then both of them sat quietly contemplating the flames, watching as they slowly flickered out.

Xanther took out some bedding from the bag that was dutifully still sitting beside him, and the two of them cuddled up together, as the last of the flames completely died out.

Xanther had started to descend to sleep when finally Beth spoke.

"I have something to tell you," she said, "It's about Luke."

He sat up, the camp now completely dark and silent around them.

"W-what is it?" he asked, a slow, confused dread filling his thoughts.

"He wasn't really my brother. That was just our disguise."

"Disguise? Tell me why you would need one," Xanther replied.

"We were running, but it felt like we were running from ghosts. I thought he was dead, you see, years ago. It seemed like he'd managed to get away and that he pretty much thought the same about me, so he didn't come to find me and my sisters.

Now, I have no sisters. I have no one." She sat up and continued, looking into eyes she could not quite see.

"It feels like I've been running forever. I had two 'sisters' and we all seemed to have our own gifts. I continually had flashes of my past from a long time ago, a secret I kept hidden from them both until the horror started.

"It started when I was much younger and I met the girls. Their family took me in to their home and I used to stare into the flames at the fireplace. It really scared the hell out of me when I heard them, the Chaka, calling my name and I stopped looking after that.

"I came here after they finally caught up with us...my sisters weren't fast enough and for some reason I was spared. We started running when they ruined our home. I knew, deep down, what that reason was and I hated myself for causing my sisters' deaths. I ran and I didn't stop, couldn't bear to look back; I travelled with barely anything to my name until I arrived in Middletown.

"I didn't know it until it was too late, but it turns out I was drawn there, by the same pull that They used to find me. I was pulled to Tristan, my love.

"I had become part of the underground community, fitting in with their everyday workload and making new friends, when one day, I saw him standing there. It took away every defence I had, every secret I'd tried to forget. It all came flooding back and disarmed everything I'd built up over the years. I approached him cautiously and then ran into his arms.

"He was the same Tristan I'd left, the same Tristan I'd tried to forget about, the same one I'd loved with every essence of what I had on this world. We had escaped together, a very long time ago... although that's not really true; I followed him. We only found each other afterwards. You know – that's what really bothers me. We kept finding each other and we loved each other, always."

After a silence, Xanther said, "You're going to have to slow down, Beth, I'm not sure I understand much of what you're saying."

"Years ago now, I escaped from a different world. I have vivid memories of that world now; it is a place of mesmerising beauty but terrible, terrible darkness and pain. I was part of 'Them', the Chaka, who sucked the life and energy out of anything vibrant and alive.

"In that world we were told a story, a myth: that two powerful guardians ruled our world long, long ago who conflicted with each other. Like most worlds, a war cast a shadow on what was a world full of life and growth. We were told that destruction won, peace was overpowered and the Guardian and her followers were consumed by hate and fire, their energy becoming the life force that flowed to make the world grow stronger."

"Wait – so what's happening now, here. You think all this may have something to do with you?"

Beth sighed, "I'm sure I am the reason for all this, yes. Before now I've been too scared to admit it. I have no doubt in my mind that they followed me here."

Xanther said, "Look, even if that is true, you're going to be safe. Everything is going to be all right." He felt the tears that were slowly falling down her cheeks and pulled her closer to him.

He lay there trying to digest all the information she had confided in him, but the truth seemed so horrible. He understood now why she seemed to hold a deep secret in her heart and why she sometimes seemed guarded.

He felt remorse as her protector, because he could not protect her from herself and her memories. Her dreams came back to hurt her every night and he could never be a part of her past like that.

She held his hand gently, her soft fingers wrapping around his slightly rough ones.

"Don't worry about me," she whispered to him, "I'm so very strong and, whatever happens, I can face this without you."

"I know, I love you," he replied, never doubting that he meant it. Her beauty shone through the terrible burden she carried on her shoulders and he felt a powerful need to take it all away.

They lay there wrapped up warmly as he stroked Beth's soft hair with his fingertips, thinking of what was to come. He realised how hard it must have been to tell him who she really was, the risk of understanding she'd taken and how much of a weight had probably lifted from her mind. The horror of what her story had meant hadn't really sunk in as he thought about his love for her.

For a while she was silent and as he drifted off into dreams he heard her say, "Please never leave me."

They fell asleep in each others arms that night, and the warmth they shared together seemed to grow.

Chapter Sixteen

Connections

The sun shone down brightly on the small paradise the colony had worked to build up over the time they had lived there, in the forest. It was mostly sheltered by trees, but the sunlight shone through as there were probably fewer trees there than in the rest of the forest. Some of them had been chopped down to make a couple of huts, but most of the members of the colony lived in strong reinforced tents and wagons. Seeing it in the daylight, Beth was amazed how easily the small community thrived here, and how friendly everybody was to her. She had awoken early that day, and just lay there beside Xanther, watching as he slept beside her, peacefully. A few other people were up, walking around and going about their usual daily business. Xanther stirred beside her, and she looked down at him adoringly.

"Good morning," she said, as she kissed him on the forehead. He yawned, and then looked up at her, eyes screwed up because of the light.

"What time is it?" Xanther asked her.

"No idea," she said, smiling and looking at her surroundings in a contented awe. "I like it here," she said to him, "It's so peaceful and nothing looks complicated."

"That's the way they like things here, darling. That's why they chose to live here in the first place," Xanther replied. He admitted to himself he liked the thought of it too. Sam came over to them and the three got talking, mostly about how they lived and the lifestyle here; none of them wanted to mention the night before so soon.

"Right, who's for breakfast?" Sam said eventually, rubbing his hands together. Beth could tell that he had missed being here and he felt happy being back with some of his old friends again. Soon, a few more people joined them and they shared breakfast together, including Brent who looked fresh eyed and eager to hear Sam's stories, after a good night's sleep. He sat down between Xanther and Sam, and Beth secretly studied him as he spoke. It was as if he knew something more about the situation than they had told him, as nobody had really brought up the events from the past night. The feeling was in the air though, and it was only a matter of time before someone would have to bring it up. Beth sighed; she didn't feel very hungry any more.

"Ermm, is it okay if I go stretch my legs for a while? I'd like to have a little explore," she said, slowly getting to her feet.

"Sure," replied Xanther, "You haven't really looked around much yet. Go ahead,"

She felt curiously refreshed as she surveyed her new surroundings; she decided to go right, towards the man-made water fountain.

Brent could feel something in the air, but decided to stay quiet as this was not the time to bring it up. Yawning, he looked around and saw Beth headed for the fountain, and to the left he saw Bryan who was fixing one of the wagons that had sprung a leak. The wagons were old and needed some maintenance from time to time, and their paint was peeling off. Brent leaned back and watched as Xanther and Sam ate breakfast, probably avoiding whatever was bothering them. Afterwards, Jared arrived with Vincent and Daire. Kordian was exploring, as usual.

"I think you'll all agree that we have quite a big problem on our hands," Jared spoke. "These so-called creatures are on the loose, and things we have been hearing up here are not good."

Xanther sat and quietly listened, watching Jared as he began to divulge the information they had learned from the traders, the dark, mysterious traders who always seemed to know everything from their travels.

"There's something going on in the Aime building. The lights are always on, yet no one seems to enter or leave, and the amount of energy generating from that place is off the scale; not something we tolerate here."

Xanther sighed, "Please tell me you're kidding... my parents used to own that company, I sold it when they died."

"And were they experimenting with lasers back then too?" Jared asked him directly.

Xanther looked stunned and all he could say was, "No, I don't think so."

"Aime?" Beth said from behind them, making them all jump as none of the party had been aware of her return.

"Yes, Aime. So they owned the company? How long ago?" asked Jared, who stared intently into Xanther's eyes, almost piercing in their intensity.

"A few years ago, before the plane crash. I sold it when I was eighteen."

"I'm not sure what is going on down there, but I can guarantee it isn't computer-related," Jared sighed.

"So what are we going to do?" asked Vincent, anxiously this time. Could it be possible that whatever was going on around them probably had something to do with that building?"

"We've got to stop it, somehow," replied Xanther thoughtfully.

"Stop it? How? Xanther, I don't want you risking your lives for those things, you or anybody else," Beth demanded, her worried eyes started into Xanther's.

"We'll need weapons," said Sam, quickly followed by a sharp sigh of dread from Beth.

"Kordian?" Freya stopped walking.

"What, honey?" he asked, turning round to look at her. He thought she looked scared.

"Do you think that the monsters will find a way into the woods?"

"Come here," he said, walking towards her and bending down so he looked into her eyes, "No monster is going to find us here." He smiled. She smiled back and the pair hugged.

The light shimmered down in rays to the ground, the large, ancient trees blocking out the rest of the light. Morning dew glistened still on their branches and leaves, making them shiny and mystical. The tall trees surrounded Kordian and Freya as they embraced, and Freya imagined this was somewhere fairies might have lived, long ago. It was entrancing, the way the light danced all around, lighting up the area around them. It made even the shadows seem warm.

Kordian didn't know the reasons for her approach, did not even hear her, but all of a sudden she was there, all the same. The next time he looked up, she was there standing in front of him, long black hair flowing, long grey dress, flimsy and torn at the bottom but perfect in its beauty. Slowly, Freya turned around to look too. What she saw was a tall lady, with perfect red lips and hair almost down to her knees. She turned slowly to Freya, and her red lips formed a perfect smile, her pale face was the colour of exquisite cream.

Kordian tried to talk, but was lost for words. She took two small steps forward. The two watched as her lips moved in some exquisite language, a whisper, forming words they could barely hear. Then she stumbled, her thin frame suddenly looking weak and he caught her before she fell.

Slowly, they began to walk back to the village.

The sunlight crept in past the heavily draped velvet, as if it could not succeed in being properly banished. Four tall figures stood over the makeshift bed of satin kindly set up by Yaira, one of the older settlers. They watched her lie there; beautiful but weak. A couple of times she muttered something in her sleep in a beautiful language they did not know.

"And she was just standing there?" asked Sam, never once taking his eyes off the girl. Jared stood silent, watching her breathe. She seemed peaceful as she slept; her long lashes fluttered from time to time but apart from that she was still.

"She whispered something before tripping; I do not know what it was. She didn't have much strength, I think she needs rest."

"And where is Freya now?" Sam said.

"She's with Beth. I saw them earlier," replied Xanther, "In fact, I'm going to check on them now."

"I'll go with you," said Sam, and the two took their leave. Jared stood there watching, as the sleeping beauty slept. Finally, Daire left also and then he was left alone. He sighed to himself, and gently stroked her brow before making sure the drapes were pulled shut behind him.

There was something about this beauty that seemed slightly familiar to him, although he had no idea how. He frowned as he looked at her now, still and silent, and most importantly so pale. Her skin was flawless, but something about her made him feel suddenly so cold.

All of a sudden, the room became much darker as if overtaken by shadow. The curtains blew softly and the light from underneath them was still there... Jared slowly backed away from the bed and left the room. Never had he felt so unwelcome in his life.

Outside, it had started to snow. A heavy blanket had covered the ground in no time at all; the kind of clean white blanket that you feel you'd like to immerse yourself in, but at the same time knowing that if you fell asleep under it, you'd freeze to death. A cold blanket that somehow made everything seem fresh and new. A robin sat high on the top of a tree, looking fat and slightly too heavy for its branch. It had been a good winter, with plenty of berries, at least in these woods.

The trees surrounding it stood proud and tall. It was almost daunting looking up at some of them. Xanther soon found Freya and Beth having a snow fight. Snow was flying everywhere, and Freya had Beth almost covered. With her small frame she looked like a snow-child and not a women of twenty three years. Laughing, she threw a snowball at Freya covering her hair and back as she ran away.

"Snow-children aren't supposed to throw snow at beautiful girls. It's rude!" he shouted, startling them both slightly. He laughed at their surprised looks, and then Beth promptly threw a snowball at him.

"We're both beautiful young women and it's rude to spy!" Beth shouted back, giggling. The snowball hit Xanther in the face.

"Hey! Right…" He started to gather up a large bundle of snow.

He stopped when Beth came near, brushing the snow out of her hair with one cold hand as she smiled. She looked radiant, her cheeks slightly red, she had a healthy glow to her now. He smiled back, completely forgetting the world around them for just that one moment.

"Well, you found us," she said.

"Yes, I certainly did. Aren't you two cold?"

"It's too much fun to be cold," giggled Freya. She was now standing between them, looking perfectly happy and healthy in only a light hooded brown jacket. Beth gave her a worried glance.

"You're right, maybe we should go back inside for a while."

"Come on then," Xanther replied whilst scooping up a barely protesting Freya, "I'll walk you back. My fingers are getting frostbite." This made Freya giggle more and the three of them stumbled through the deep snow, already thinking about the warm fire that would welcome them back.

When they did find their way back, everything was quiet and exactly the way they had left it. The cold air seemed to disintegrate around the fire, and there sat Jared, wise as ever, waiting for their return.

He looked somewhat tired but calmer and more settled than when Xanther had left. Jared was not the sort of person to show his feelings on the outside, but earlier he had looked… troubled.

The night was coming fast now, and the darkness surrounded them outside the bright fire. The woods were full of shadows at night, and it was hard to tell what occupied them. When dark comes everything stays the same, really. It's just the imagination that runs wild, and makes monsters out of darkness and night; shadows that disappear with the coming of the day. But in these woods, it is much wiser to stay around others, as creatures of the night lurk.

It was later that night when Jared announced to the group that he had called for an old acquaintance.

"Nothing else should be decided until he gets here," he informed them. "Hopefully he will have information to help us with our decision, but first, tell me something." He turned to Sam. "What makes you think you can stop this?"

Sam, who had spent most of the day in thought about this, now looked back at his old friend.

"We have to because someone has to. I'm not hiding in fear of those things, or the people behind it; I want to know why this happened."

"You never were one to stand by and watch," smiled Jared.

"You know I was never a coward either," replied Sam. He looked to his brothers for support, as they were all beside him now. Middletown was their home. It stood for everything they had and they were not going to allow it to be ripped apart by anything, even if it was something they didn't understand.

"We have to go back, we can't just leave things the way they are." Everyone turned to Xanther. He was right. That was the simplest answer. "Everything was in chaos back there, and I'm worried it's so quiet," Xanther explained. This made them all stop. It had been quiet, but it's normally so peaceful anyway so far from the town. It could mean anything.

Jared's old friend, Lucian arrived late that night. Beth was woken by his arrival. She lay on her back, half-looking up at the old wood above her, listening. Many greetings prevailed, Jared's being the loudest. Beth, surrounded by a hazy mist of sleep, half heard the meeting begin. Slowly she drifted off, their voices forgotten by the next day.

They had gathered around the large rock upon which Lucian sat. He had much to say and happily announced that fact.

His long white hair flowed down past his shoulders and almost blended into the elegant blue velvet cloak that covered him regally. His eyes were a bright purple in colour and most striking, his face younger than expected with very few wrinkles and a smile.

Xanther had slowly made his way over to join the rest, and none of the settlers seemed to mind, or even notice him being there. Beth had not noticed his disappearance when she woke, and now he wanted to be back with her again. There was an odd sort of coldness around them, and the conversation had dulled considerably since Lucian's arrival, hushed tones barely audible so as not to be heard by the sleeping ones. Lucian, in many ways resembled Jared – old, respectable looking with a great sense of depth. His presence dominated the small crowd, the select few.

"It has begun." Lucian watched the faces as they listened. "I've felt it for a long time. With dread I've tried to figure out what it was."

Xanther felt himself turn to ice as Lucian continued.

I know what is happening but I never thought it would happen in this lifetime. I have only heard of these creatures in old myths that were told to me by my forefathers, passed down for generations."

"I recognise these... creatures. They have malicious intent. The Chaka, a remnant race from an ancient civilisation have sent these creatures to us, which means that the Chaka themselves will soon follow."

"What is this civilisation? Where are they from and why haven't we heard of them?" asked Sam.

Lucian slowly turned his gaze on Sam, "Let me explain. The Chaka are from a dark and forbidding otherworld, somewhere strange and alien to our eyes. They made it the hell that it is and I'm afraid if they come through to this one, they will do the very same here."

"The beasts are called raghuals. They are solid yet not, they use the air rather than legs and they suck out the souls of the living. Blood makes them stronger, builds up their mass but they have no real need for substance to live."

No one dared to speak a word. They listened as he continued.

"I have felt this presence slowly building, the channel between their world and ours perhaps becoming progressively weaker by the day. I believe they are working up to something and they will get what they came for unless we find a way to stop them; they are not from this world. Not quite alive and not quite dead, they are feeding on the souls of the living. First we need to figure out what they want or what they are here to collect."

The circle paused for thought, each member taking in this information silently, in their own way.

The wind seemed to slow, Lucian's head was lowered with eyes closed, and peacefully time seemed to stop all around the circle.

Xanther could feel his heart heavy in his chest, and all he could think of was Beth; he had many questions. What if Beth was part of all this?

All of a sudden the mood was broken and Lucian's head snapped up, eyes wide open, he uttered these words, "You leave first thing. Make haste for the festival or else many lives will be lost."

Chapter Seventeen

Garas Camp

Fireworks blasted up into the dark sky, violently lighting up the dusky desert backdrop as the crowds below cried in joy and celebration. Adults and children danced to the music and drinks were flowing. Belly dancers moved exotically and leather-clad bikers stared up at the fireworks, sipping beer from their tankards. Two days before Mallia festival marked the celebration of the small desert camp, before everything was packed up and the travel to Middletown began. The travellers attended the festival every year and this year would be no different.

The camp was established by the Garas, in the desert wasteland south-east of Middletown and close to the dried out city of Bryian, where Billy had travelled from Bryian.

The band played familiar songs to the enjoyment of many younglings, and Billy sneered from the sidelines; this wasn't his type of music at all. It was simple and out-of-tune to his alien ears, and he smiled as he remembered his attempt at that lonely bar.

He took a deep breath that smelled of smoke before entering the crowd. He was looking for someone in particular, and hoped the dirty travellers would be able to help him to find who he was looking for.

A young celebrating couple ran in front of his path and then stopped abruptly when they noticed the pale-looking bald rogue with the bright blue eyes and the bitter look of malice on his face.

Curious, one spoke, "Hi there, are you here for the party?"

"Lucian," Billy growled. The couple simply looked at each other without recognition, and Billy trod forward, almost knocking the boy over.

"Hey, watch it!" the young man shouted.

Billy turned and shot a look that turned the young man's blood to ice, and he quickly pulled his girlfriend back into the crowd.

Billy pounded forward and kicking over a barrel he made his way to one of the tents and ripped back the opening. Not stopping, he stepped inside and was confronted by three people.

"Lucian," Billy growled. "He was here not long ago."

An older gentleman, dressed in blue satin robes was the first to speak, "I do not know why you have come here, but please leave. No one of that name lives here."

"I can smell his scent," Billy spoke in a low voice; his expression was one full of hatred. He was met by silence.

"Where is he?" Billy demanded, startling the older man.

One of the younger men stepped forward and held out his arm. Billy shot a glance at the man and using his mind, threw him off his feet where he crashed against the wall of the tent with force.

The intruder then stepped forward with malevolence towards the old man, grabbed him firmly by the neck and spoke very calmly, with barely a whisper, "I'm going to ask you once more."

He was interrupted by the third tent occupant, who tried to approach Billy, "No!" the man shouted. He stopped abruptly and felt his chest, a look of horror on his face, before he burst into flames.

"He's not here," the old man wavered. "I think he went to Middletown to help prepare for Mallia. Please, I beg of you, leave here, demon."

A deep, warped laugh started to emanate from Billy's stomach up into his throat and out of his twisted smile. He dropped the elderly gent with force and stormed out of the tent.

The crowd now made room for him, faces looking on in fear. The music had stopped and a couple of children started to cry.

Billy stared only at the space in front of him as he stormed over to a powerful motorbike that had caught his eye. The owner dared not to argue as the leather-clad malevolent force sped off into the night, in the direction of the nearest main town, leaving nothing behind but smoke.

Chapter Eighteen

Ulla's Choice

It was early morning in Fahra Point when Beth arose from her slumber to many voices and sounds. Slipping out of bed and covering herself in a large throw, her head felt like cotton wool. She shivered and cautiously stepped out of the wagon.

To her confusion, many people were packing up, including Xanther and the brothers. They were accompanied by Brent and a group of settlers, who took the journey each year to travel to Mallia festival.

Mallia was the biggest celebration in West Orenia, a festival of light and music, fun and the heart of individuality which took place in the underground of Middletown.

Travellers came from all corners of the world to take part in celebrations which grew each year, and, for around a week, the underground was filled with bright, colourfully dressed punters, face-painted performers and serene, powerful and spiritual music all blended into one another.

But for the brothers, Mallia held a sense of dread this year as they returned to the town which they'd fled only days before.

Beth tiptoed into the packing group and was first noticed by Vincent, "Hey, you're up," he said smiling. "Thought we'd have to come and wake you."

"What's going on?" she asked.

Xanther turned to face her, "We're going back, along with these guys," he told her, gesturing to the settlers and their backpacks. "They're travelling to the festival and agreed to accompany us on our way."

Brent was sitting on one of the rocks, sharpening his blade in preparation for the thick forests.

"All right," said Beth, "When are we leaving?"

"Beth, you should stay and look after Freya. It could be dangerous back there," Sam replied.

She turned to Xanther, "I'm not leaving you! I'm just as good to fight, I'm coming with you."

Xanther paused, trying to gather his thoughts and to hide his fear for Beth. He walked over to her, his arms rested on her shoulders and looked gently into her determined eyes, "Okay then, come. But remember, we don't know what we're going to find. You're cold – go and pack."

She nodded, kissed him and then turned to the rest of the group when the wind started. It sounded like a force had hit the forest, hurtling through the trees and branches like a small hurricane. It blew throughout the camp and made them cold to the bone. Then it happened.

The beasts rushed through the camp, their awful roars sounding like terrible death and pain, high pitched yet terrible. Bits of forest, fabric and devastation flew around the camp and all the group could do was crouch down, hands over their ears. Wagons smashed, tents ripped and from behind them came a chanting grew progressively louder; it was Jared.

One of the beasts turned to him, un-repelled by his spells it roared a terrible sound and almost seemed to encase the tall figure of Jared, who stood strong against its force.

The beast seemed to be drawing in his strength, and Jared started to scream although it was like he was screaming within a bell jar.

Beth, her hands over her head could barely make out what was happening, but it looked like the essence of the man was being pulled out like smoke, his face stretched and pained, his very soul being sucked out of its shell. She screamed but no sound seemed to come out. She could barely breathe.

Jared's body fell like a heap to the ground and shots were fired into the beast. Snapping round, it focused on Vincent who was holding the gun. Through the mini hurricane it advanced upon the young man, joined by another. The first beast seemed to claw the second and the first roared loudly.

The wind had grown to almost unbearable levels when suddenly roars of what could only be inhuman pain emanated from around them. Beth realised it could only be the beasts, and suddenly the wind stopped.

The small, crouching figures vaguely made out the two beasts in suspended animation. They seemed to be getting thinner, their bodies breaking up into dust and rising up like ashes.

Xanther, eyes half open could make out a third now too, rising from within the forest. Suddenly the dust broke up into the air and was gone.

Brent, without hesitation ran over to the crumpled heap that was Jared.

The rest turned to look at the figure that was now solid in-between the two tents. Tall and striking she stood, her long black hair and floor-length grey gown blowing in the gentle breeze. It was the same beautiful figure they had witnessed in a deep sleep, but now she stood before them.

Her hand slowly raised and a golden energy seemed to flow from her, across the devastation the beasts had caused, as she approached the blue cloaked figure which lay on the floor.

"No!" shouted Brent, but not before the figure of the old man started to rise into the air. It was Lucian.

Her energy continued to rotate the old man and his frailty struck Xanther for the first time. It was then that Lucian started to move slowly, and soon he was standing up, feet firmly on the ground. The golden energy flashed back into the unknown yet ethereal woman and with that, she fell violently to the ground.

Rays of sunlight started to break down onto the crumpled grey mesh of her dress, while the small speechless crowd slowly gathered around her.

Lucian knelt down beside her and spoke softly, "What is your name, child?"

She uttered one word before falling into sleep, "Ulla."

Chapter Nineteen

The Water

The settlers led the group deeper north into the forest. Pushing ever forward they knew the names of every tree and plant, every sound. With regards to the situation, they mostly kept themselves to themselves, although they were armed with care.

They seemed to walk for hours, sheltered from the sun by the thick forest around them. Now and again rays of sunlight shone down, looking magical.

Beth could tell that Sam was worried about leaving Freya at the settlement, but the walk alone was too much for a child, never mind the approaching danger. She hesitated slightly, as the guilt hit her hard. She reached for the amulet around her neck; she only hoped she had the strength within to overcome the Chaka.

The old fear, never really gone from her mind welled up deep within her now, overtaking rational thoughts whenever she let it. She had to face this fear.

Xanther smiled at her, his hand resting gently on her shoulder.

"Are you all right?" he asked.

She smiled back, and said, "Yeah, just gathering my thoughts."

It was early evening when up ahead the group seemed to have stopped. The forest had been getting thinner for the last couple of minutes and then she saw why; a lake glistened calmly ahead of them, whose beauty took her breath away as they all gathered in awe.

"The Konache lake, men and women," said Brent. "Our ancestors worshipped this lake many years ago. We always acknowledge it as we pass."

"I had no idea," whispered Beth.

"Neither had I," Xanther spoke softly. A slight mist hung over the lake although the water looked almost alive in its brightness.

Sam and Daire had come to rest on the edge of the grass, both looking out onto the water; there was a calmness about them that Beth had never witnessed before. She realised she could feel it within her too. A weight somehow lifted from her shoulders.

She reached out and touched Xanther, who jumped slightly, as if awakening from a dream.

"Look at it," he said, "It's wishing us well." She smiled, wondering if it was true. It was funny; the dark oasis of the lake had stopped everyone dead in their tracks, even Sam, the most turbulent.

Brent said, "Let's rest for a while before we set up camp." Everyone agreed.

With bare feet, she ran down through the long cold grass, back towards the lake. The settlers had set up camp further ahead, where they were determined to spend the night, and after a long, almost peaceful discussion it seemed like they'd almost forgotten the worry they faced returning to the town. But Beth had not forgotten. The feelings haunted her waking moments like a bad nightmare.

She asked herself what good she could possibly do here. Perhaps the best move would be to disappear altogether. She thought of Xanther, asleep beside the embers of the fire as she silently crept out of the bedding and she blinked away the tears that were starting to form in her eyes. This was no night to enjoy the pleasures that life normally gave her so abundantly, or used to.

She looked up at the moon as she ran, slightly breathless now. The moon looked down on her like an old friend, full and white. The music and laughing were in the distance in the back of her mind now, ahead of her; the lake. She sighed as her feet touched the cool pebbles.

Her pace slowed as she followed the small path overgrown with plants that led to the lake. It protected her from light; she gently stepped over the plants as she had done so many times before, idly picking at bits of leaves or flowers. This time was different, and she sang ever so softly under her breath as she pushed the small, tender branches out of the way.

It wasn't long until the path opened out in front of her and the moon flooded over the beautiful dark water. The feelings inside her rose up and intermixed, feelings of being stifled, of fear and of a deep sadness that had been within her for many months now. She felt herself relax as she breathed in deeply, feeling the sand between her toes. She smiled.

She found herself walking through the pale hard pebbles, feeling them beneath her feet, she savoured the cool breeze and once again looking up at the moon. Pausing, as the cold water gently trickled around her feet, she pulled her dress up over her head, discarded it behind her. The air on her naked skin felt so good, and she began to step into the water without looking behind.

The water felt cool as she waded, almost in a trance deeper and deeper towards the lake, the water looked dark and forbidding. The moon illuminated her pale skin and she thought of nothing now: the feeling was too good to think.

It became too deep; Beth plunged with pleasure into the dark, cool waters and started to swim. The coolness touched her long hair and she closed her eyes before looking up again at the moon, beautiful, shining down like the one solid thing in her world. The water made ripples around her, and still she swam ever forward.

Her feelings flooded into her mind like the water all around her, dark and liquid, and all she wanted to do was swim.

She swam until her legs felt heavy and her arms like rubber; still she swam. Not once did she turn her head, the water splashing up and mixing with her tears. She made herself swim, her breath increasing with lake water sometimes leaking into her mouth, causing her to recoil slightly.

Her memories blended into one, sad feeling and her mind was once again filled with the happiness of what her life could have been like, if she were normal. It was getting cold now; she felt her body start to shiver perhaps from the water, perhaps from tiredness. Idly she grasped the moonstone ring on her finger, dropped it deep into the water. She felt so free.

Her muscles were increasing their ache and the feeling of tiredness gradually began to take over her. It would be time to stop swimming soon, time to let go. Listening to the silence around her, she took in one last breath before she finally stopped; tired and heavy she let herself sink. The moon shone up from under the waves and she smiled as her vision became blurred and her eyes finally closed.

She sensed the presence before she saw it, rising up from the water and gently embracing her like a warm womb. Opening her eyes she was met with something too bright to make out. Her senses flooding with calm she reached out, feeling the smooth almost not-quite-there figure.

Suddenly her body was jerked upwards, firms hands clasped around her waist and she was ascending again. She couldn't struggle, confusion filled her mind and then fresh air once again filled her lungs. She gasped in shock; Xanther was holding her as he struggled for breath.

"Why?" She breathed, shivering in the cold of the night.

"You're asking me that?" Xanther asked. Now able to look into her eyes he saw that her heart was full of pain. Still recovering, she answered with silence, eyes looking down under the water.

Xanther continued, "Okay, we're going to swim to shore now. I'll help you. One, two, three…"

The couple reached the bank a few minutes later, shaken and chilled to the bone. She could barely see his black eyes in the night sky but she saw them shining. Shivering, he held her close to him as they lay under the moon, exhausted and overwhelmed.

"I can't do this, Xanther… you're all in danger and it's all because of me," she whispered.

"That's not true. Shhhh," he answered her, trying to comfort her but inside he knew he was scared.

She awoke in the tent, warm next to the small fire. He lay next to her, watching her with sleepy eyes.

"Why did you do that?" he asked, stroking her hair. He looked concerned, his eyes full of love for her.

"They want me, Xanther. I thought I'd be more useful to you dead."

He held her tightly, his face wet with tears and she could tell she'd hurt him in the most stupid way possible. She had no idea how to repair what she had done.

She kissed him, reached out for him and the lovers grew warmer together. He kissed her tears away and they made love until it felt like they were just the one person, never to be separated. It made her feel warm as if she had found her destiny in him. She realised he was everything she could ever want, as she rested in his strong loving arms.

They fell asleep, silently as the fire slowly stopped burning. They slept, bound together until late morning.

It was late at night and dark in the underground unit as Raoul stared coldly into the mirror. His eyes were a dark brown; his deeply tanned skin looked bronze in the darkness of the mirror. He had a skinny frame, with considerable muscles that had come as a result of a lot of work at the gym. He wore a white vest and black jeans which accentuated his slender body.

He knew the Wolf would come for them all soon. He sighed and tried to tell himself he didn't care but deep down he stored a bad feeling in his gut. It had been there for a while, each time he heard the low growl from his mobile phone.

Violently slamming his fist into the mirror, he watched it shatter into tiny pieces which landed on the floor. He looked absently at the blood on his hand, disgusted at his own weakness.

Chapter Twenty

Mallia

The underground was teeming with colours and sounds. People crowded through the walkways by the thousands to join the first of the celebrations. It was the first day of Middletown's biggest and only event, Mallia.

It was hard to tell people apart in the sway of colourful hats, masks and fancy dress many of them wore as part of the festival tradition.

Street performers stood by the sidelines and corners of the main corridors, giving out balloons, telling jokes and charming the audiences with their tricks.

Music poured into the crowd from every shop and bar, and revellers ran in and out celebrating drunkenly with one another.

Even some of the last-surviving elders of Middletown joined in on the fun in the same way as new residents of the underground. Mallia was something they were unable to ignore since the noise of the festival drowning out every television set.

There had been rumours of the government sending riot officers to control the crowds, but many believed this would do more harm than good and guards stood at every gate entrance. Even some of the gangs had offered to help stand guard to prevent officials from storming the grounds and walkways under Middletown.

Uncle watched lovingly as two of his young nephews played with one of the performers in the crowd. The Red was full of diners and party-goers, all adding to the atmosphere of the festival. The old man was so rushed off his feet that he'd had to call in extra reinforcements.

A performer stood with a face painted white with pink, green and blue spots spaced around his striking features. A colourful jester hat sat atop his head, slightly scrunched and not quite straight. A small table stood in front of him and balanced on the table were cups and one single red rubber ball. His voice was loud and cocky as he announced what he planned to do.

"Come on, you lot. I bet you can't find where the ball goes! Roll up and watch closely, sires, or else you'll lose in no time!"

The jester twirled the cups in the air like a barman, as he accepted the bets. Time seemed to move slowly as they span in mid-air, before he caught them causing the audience to applaud louder.

"Now watch," he said, beginning to demonstrate how the game worked. The idea was not an uncommon one, an old trick often seen at fairgrounds and travelling circuses around Orenia. The rubber ball would be placed under one of the three cups, the cups would be mixed up quickly until the eye could not spot which cup the ball was under. It was then that the player made his choice. This game required a quick eye, or so one would have thought.

When the cups came to a standstill, the jester pointed to a young boy to the side of him. He asked him, "Now, where is the ball, young man? Do you know?"

The boy smiled and shouted, "Yes!" The jester made a point of wiping his forehead, and gestured for the boy to come closer.

"Well, point out which it is then!" The boy pointed to the cup on the right, before looking hesitantly at the performer. The performer nodded, and the boy picked up the cup to reveal the red ball, making the game look easy. The audience clapped.

"Now, who wants to start the game!" exclaimed the jester, eyeing up the small crowd which had now gathered around him.

"You want to play, sir?" The jester asked a boy of about sixteen at the front of the crowd. He nodded, placing his money on the table.

"Goody," said the jester, "Now watch the ball." He placed the rubber ball under the middle cup, and began to mix and muddle the cups. Progressively, the cups got faster as the jester span them around the small table, the young man's attention focusing hard on the cups until they eventually halted. The jester lifted his head and his eyes flashed gold as they met with the boy's. The boy did not falter, pointing to the cup on the right with a surety and arrogance that came along with his age.

"It's under that one," he said. The crowd watched with authority as the boy's hand reached out to uncover the cup, to find it empty. The crowd laughed as the jester picked up the middle and left cups, to watch the ball exposed from its hiding place on the left.

The jester's eye was momentarily taken by a beautiful lady pushing past the crowds, her long dark hair shining under the lights. She wore a green satin dress, bespoke with golden coinage which jangled as she walked without even a passing glance at the stall.

She walked further down the passage and stopped to greet Amos, the skinny comedian with long dark dreadlocks, who kissed her softly on the cheek.

Queues were forming around the ticket sellers, ready for the night's shows which would involve everything from comedy and music to drama and theatre. The number of shows increased each year, most of them taking place in small crowded venues with hardly more props than a few plant pots and an audience; that was the fun of the festival, not trying too hard.

The street acts were also free, with donation pots for anyone who enjoyed the performance. Money was optional and did not mean much at Mallia.

Near the south entrance, a sword eater began to assemble his show; he had wild Mohican style hair, gelled rigid and his skinny frame was topless. On his lower half he wore huge baggy jeans, ripped at the knees and down one of the thighs.

Outside, Billy stood a few feet away from the South Gate entrance. Above ground the air had only started to darken. He needed no refuge from the dull, mid-morning sky. His dirty clothes blew in the cold fresh air.

He sensed the presence of the raghuals nearby, probably awakening from their daytime slumber. He knew that their darkness would be drawn to him, their senses sharp and keen to their master.

He watched as a young guard opened the gate for three of the brightly-dressed revellers and decided it was almost time to make his entrance.

He measured up and down the streets, walking quickly down the slope to the South Gate entrance. It was mostly silent around the town; the way he liked it, but he guessed that most had probably flocked underground like sheep.

As he approached the gate, the guard eyed the ragged character suspiciously. His trousers were almost in shreds, his black t-shirt was dusty from travelling and it was obvious he was carrying weapons; not that it was rare in these times.

The young guard started the door mechanism as Billy got nearer. He said, "Hi, all right?"

Billy replied, "I'm just excellent, thank you."

The heavy gate slowly retracted, creating a large gap in the underground entrance. He started to step through, eyes drawn to the masses of spectators inside the grounds. Their noise almost hurt his sensitive ears as he entered. Before the door could properly shut, his feet came to a halt. He turned sharply to see a black shape rapidly approaching the closing gate; a raghual.

The beast shrieked proudly, the noise of home somehow too familiar to his ears. It was bigger than he had expected, grown in mass mostly due to its thirst for blood. He reached for his gun, without thought. The sight of the raghual triggered something in Billy, although he couldn't figure out where it stirred inside him.

Through the small gap in the steel doors it entered, soaring above the crowds as many onlookers stood shocked and scared before it turned and headed back towards Billy.

Without hesitation he held out his arm, using his force to stop it dead in the air. It tried to fight but Billy was too strong, and the beast fell apart into tiny pieces, dissolving into the air.

The crowd were staring at Billy the beast killer, something he was not used to dealing with. Holstering the gun that he had no need to use, he looked at the ground deciding how to proceed. Eventually, expressionless he walked forward into his former audience, receiving a few wary looks but mostly attempts to approach him. He'd been labelled as a hero. The sword eater had been holding his sword protectively; he now put it back to rest on its blanket, ready for the next show. He saluted Billy who forced a small cold smile. Slowly, the noise built up again as the shaken revellers started to return to their festival, unsure whether what they've witnessed was nothing more than a publicity stunt.

As he moved through the crowd, blending in with the faces and colours he took out his black cell phone. With a swift press of the buttons and a smile forming on his face, he uttered two words, "Time's short." Slipping the phone back into his pocket he headed deeper into the underground.

Billy's 'gang-for-hire' had been based in what used to be a storeroom in the lower levels of the underground. It was little more than a cemented square room, with small rooms above used as bunks for sleeping in. The door was reinforced with steel and was usually locked.

Timmon was climbing down the rungs to the lower level walkway when suddenly he felt cold. He could hear hard footsteps walking harshly below him, nearing their headquarters.

He froze dead still in the fire shaft, listening as Billy got nearer to the door and, without hesitating, kicked it open with superhuman strength. The door loudly crumpled to the floor.

Billy came face-to-face with Raoul, who quickly grabbed his gun from the table and fired a shot into Billy's chest. With barely a moment's thought Billy forced him back against the wall, taking the gun and slamming it against Raoul's head.

He then grabbed part of the ruined door and forced it into Raoul's torso, pinning him to the wall. Blood spurted out of Raoul's chest and mouth and Billy uttered a low, guttural laugh. He turned just in time to grab Neil by the neck, squeezing hard. Neil tried to make a sound but couldn't. The veins now visible on his neck they looked appetising to Billy.

Without warning he sunk his teeth into Neil's veins, violently sucking the blood that streamed out, his hunger overwhelming him. Blood trickled down Neil's body and onto the concrete, before Billy threw the limp body to the floor.

Vesrah screamed. Her katana caught Billy's eye as she raised it above his head. Her blonde hair hung over her face and her dark blue eyes pierced his but he was too powerful. He moved faster than her eyes could take in as he grabbed the blade and cut diagonally across her body, licking the blood that oozed out of her like a river.

Her screams came to an abrupt gurgle that chilled Timmon's blood. He'd heard the whole thing, and began to climb upwards out of the fire shaft and back to the crowd of the festival.

Chapter Twenty-One

Lucian watched over her as she slept peacefully, undisturbed by the movements of the settlers outside.

"You gave me no choice," he whispered, his confusion audible. He sat hunched over, awaiting news of the travellers who'd left for Mallia. The light shone through the curtains in rays, catching the shine of the jewelled emblem, an ancient symbol of his heritage.

He turned as Freya entered the cabin, letting the sunlight fall into the room before she closed the heavy canvas door. She wore a long rough cotton smock dress, a gift from one of the settlers. Her long blonde hair was shiny from its recent wash in the river.

"Why can't she stay awake?" asked Freya, as she kneeled down by Ulla, her long dark hair mimicking a shiny waterfall over her pillow. She was once again far away in a deep sleep.

"Because," Lucian replied, "She has used up every sap of energy she had on those beasts. The poor thing has been through the wars, by the looks of it."

He held her hand softly as she slept; once again surrounded by the beautiful velvet drapes and tapestries she'd been placed in. She slept silently, never once making a sound as if her spirit had left her body and she was once more an empty shell.

This was not quite true, as the night before she had been stormy, struggling and every so often muttering in a strange but beautiful language. When darkness had well and truly fallen, Freya had heard her voice pulling her out of her slumber. It was alien-sounding to the young girl's ears and she knew some of the settlers were discussing what to do with the woman, how to bring her out of the sickness.

Back in the canvas room, all was calm as if the night before had been a forgotten nightmare.

"She's not one of us, is she Lucian?" Freya asked him. He looked at her briefly, then down at his old hands as he prepared a glass of water for the girl.

"No, not one of us," he replied swiftly, standing to his feet and motioning her out of the quarters. She could tell from the glance in his eyes that he knew something more; perhaps dangerous, that he could only keep to himself.

Her thoughts drifted to Beth and the others, probably approaching the festival by now. She wished they'd let her travel alongside them, but they'd told her it was too dangerous and she was too young to protect herself.

If circumstances were different, she might have felt bitter; this would have been her first Mallia festival.

She thought that Ulla was a pretty name, unusual. Her hand carefully brushed a strand of dark hair from Ulla's face before jumping back in surprise. Her eyes had started to flicker as if waking up from a dream.

Lucian stood to his feet and dramatically motioned Freya to leave the cabin, shouting, "Leave now, child. Fetch Mahrie and the others!"

She ran obediently from the door, glancing back once more to see bright purple eyes looking back at her.

Lucian passed Ulla the water, and fragilely she took it from his hand. He opened his mouth to speak but could not find the words, her beauty striking him speechless.

Soon he was joined by four of the Fahre Point settlers, who all looked stunned as they saw Ulla sitting up with the glass of water in her shaky hands.

"So she is real..." murmured Hasra, one of the male settlers.

"How are ye, love?" asked Mahrie, before turning to Lucian.

"Has she spoken yet?" she asked.

Lucian replied cautiously, "No, she hasn't. I don't even know if she understands what we're saying."

As if in response to his statement, Ulla slowly began to stand, placing the glass on the table beside her, her head raised high as she slowly walked towards the settlers who created a path for her. She found the door and stepped out into the sunlight, first raising her hand as if it pained her eyes.

As they came to the end of the forest that started to filter out into the town, Beth walked alongside the settlers of Fahra Point. She sensed the presence of something that had not been there before. It wasn't a good feeling, yet somehow familiar like a memory she had stored deep inside her soul. The presence seemed fuzzy, but somehow she knew it was male; that he was male.

It was early afternoon as they reached the paved ground and they emerged surrounded by a rural estate. It was unusually quiet, apart from a few children who played in the streets.

It was dull with barely any wind, the atmosphere pregnant with silence as if the calm before a storm. The air felt thick with moisture and clouds were dark in the sky.

"So this is it," Beth said, "Everything... looks normal."

Xanther glanced at her. He replied, "So far, yes. But if something's going to happen at the festival we need to get there fast."

168

Xanther had kept Beth's secret, but his fear heightened for her as they grew closer to the festival and to whatever was waiting for them.

Sam and Daire had joined them, watching the bare streets and assessing the calm.

Sam looked over at Vincent who was just emerging from the forest, followed by Kordian.

Brent turned to the group, announcing, "It is here we must leave you, friends. We wish you well with this trouble and if you need help, we'll be there."

They said goodbye and headed towards the houses on the edge of the town.

"So, now what do we do?" Xanther asked.

"Now? We need to keep moving," replied Sam.

Chapter Twenty-Two

Reaching the Gate

The doors to the West Gate entrance slowly ground shut behind them as they entered the underground. Xanther was shocked by the brightness and sheer number of people that occupied the walkways below them, as Beth took his hand and led him down the ramp into the crowd.

So many faces stood out in the crowd, and he heard Beth speak under her breath, "He's here." He looked at her, momentarily confused.

"Is he one of them?" She nodded in reply, subconsciously biting her lower lip. Sam and the others followed closely behind them, and Sam stopped him.

"We're going to find Neil," he told Xanther, "Look after her, okay?"

"Don't worry," Xanther replied, squeezing Beth's hand as the worry showed on his face; he held it back and could feel it sinking back down to the pit of his stomach.

The concentration on Beth's face showed that she was focusing on something, probably deep in the underground. He could tell that her senses were wide awake and it scared him slightly.

He saw Vincent gesture 'see you later' as he disappea into the crowd with Sam and the others. Soon they were out of sight; unexplainably he felt a loss as he watched the festival goers. He entered into the crowd with Beth, determined not to let go of his love.

Sam and Vincent grabbed the lift just in time to get to sub-level two, Neil & Co's den. The elevator was little more than a steel cage, placed by some of the early refugees who started the underground community. It made Sam feel claustrophobic. The cables badly needed oiled.

Many of the residents lived in sub-levels of the underground, three in total. It was much quieter than the walkways above, where the main festival took place.

They arrived on the floor at Unit 0033. If Sam's memory was right they would be on 0059, which wasn't far.

He started to march down the corridor, followed swiftly by Vincent before stopping at 0057.

Vincent, perplexed asked him, "Hey, what's wrong?"

"Something's not right," Sam replied, "Look at the door, it's broken."

Vincent's heart seemed to stop in his chest. Taking a step closer he saw the beginning of the mess in the small room. He caught sight of the blood.

"Oh fuck…" he said, allowing Sam to enter first. When he saw what was inside, he felt sick. Blood lined the walls; all three of them were dead. Sam looked in amazement as he saw part of the steel-reinforced door had been lifted and jammed into the wall, impaling one of the men with what must have been terrible force.

"Who could have done this?" he whispered under his breath.

Vincent, having worked up the strength to speak again replied, "I don't know, but I want to get out of here."

Just then, they heard footsteps behind them. Sam pulled out his gun and turned to find Timmon, shaky and weak in the doorway.

"No!" he shouted, tears streaming down his face as he looked around the room. He backed out slowly, and then ran towards the fire hatch. Vincent ran after him as Sam glanced round the room one more time. He cursed under his breath before running after his younger brother.

Timmon frantically climbed the rungs of the ladder and was already a quarter of the way up when Vincent climbed into the hatch, followed closely by Sam. Their steps echoed loudly in the vertical tunnel, and Timmon disappeared from view into one of the ventilation shafts above.

Vincent managed to grab hold of his trainer, as the escapee struggled in the shaft.

"Timmon!" Vincent called, "Tell us what the hell's going on!"

"Let me go!" was the reply, echoing from inside the shaft, his trainer coming loose from Vincent's grip.

"Vincent, no! Leave it!" cried Sam as Vincent climbed in after the boy, paying no heed to his brother's advice.

When Sam reached the shaft entrance he really didn't want to follow. He always found those things claustrophobic; the fire hatch was really bad enough. On the other hand, knowing his brother could be in trouble he had no other choice. Sighing, he took a deep breath and climbed into the shaft entrance.

He was definitely of bigger build than both of the boys, and the size of the shaft intimidated him.

"Why am I doing this…" he whispered under his breath. As quickly as he could, he navigated the shaft, his heart beating faster by the minute. The sounds echoed through the shaft and Sam could feel the vibrations around it. It didn't help his courage and neither did the screams to follow.

As the shaft opened out into a small room, he saw Vincent had cornered the hysterical Timmon.

He was screaming, "Get away! Don't kill me, please. I didn't know. Leave me alone!"

Sam crawled to the opposite corner, as Vincent turned to him with a confused look on his face.

"What is he talking about?" he asked.

Sam shrugged, "The kid looks terrified." He turned to Timmon, who was trembling all over.

"Who did this?" Sam asked.

"It was B-Billy, I don't want to die. Please help," Timmon stuttered.

Vincent turned to Sam and mouthed *who's Billy*, Sam shook his head. They were right below the main festival on the top floor. The underground levels were well-ventilated, with shafts running between all the levels crossing over each other.

Sometimes they served as a good escape route for anyone who was in trouble, although Sam had never really used them himself. However there was something that stood out to him, something that looked like it didn't belong. It was placed in the corner of the small metal room, above Timmon's head.

"He killed them," Timmon continued, "They're all dead and he's going to kill everyone. We thought he was one of us but now I don't know why he's here or what he's looking for."

Sam didn't really take in Vincent's questions, his mind now wandering to the strange-looking mechanism on the ceiling. Vincent was talking, "And how do you know where he is now?"

"He's here," Timmon replied, "He's waiting for something."

"Waiting for what?" Vincent demanded.

Timmon shouted back, "I don't know! I don't fucking know all right! All I know is this place is history in around thirty-three minutes."

"It's a bomb, isn't it? The whole place is littered with bombs…" They turned to look at Sam, who was staring up at the wall. Vincent followed his gaze, then jumped as his eyes focused on the small device.

"Uh-huh," Timmon replied, "I helped set them up. There's too many to stop it now."

"Shit," Sam muttered.

Above them and not far away, Xanther would not take his eyes off Beth as they walked deeper into the festival. Not long ago he would never have dreamed of being around so many people, but as long as he had her he could handle it.

Uneasily he looked around the crowd at the masked faces and brightly-coloured hats. He realised that the person or thing they were looking for could be any one of these characters around him. It gave him the creeps.

Beth wore an elegant midnight blue dress, draping loosely from her slight frame, the low back accompanied by a large blue sash that hung low. Her knee-high black leather boots worked well with the outfit, and her long brown hair shone under the low lights.

She got many looks as they walked passed the thousands of people who were celebrating the peak of the festival. The attention only made Xanther paranoid. Although he had a weapon he did not know how to protect her from what she was about to face. *The Chaka,* he thought, could harness so much more power than he could probably understand.

The noise and commotion was starting to make his head feel weak and dizzy, the voices echoing into each other and becoming one voice; it hurt his head. He started to feel a dull ache at his temples and his vision blurred slightly, making him stumble.

Beth noticed right away and stopped him, holding his arm and standing close to him in case he should fall. She looked into his eyes, which looked distressed.

"What is it? Is it him?" she asked, concerned.

"I don't know..." he replied, as she pushed her body against his and hugged him, protecting him from the crowd. Her warmth seemed to spread through his body and slowly he felt clearer.

"*How are you doing this*," he whispered.

"You're not clear right now. Try and focus and it will all go away," she spoke softly in his ear.

He focused on the individual noises of the crowd, their smiles and movements and his vision seemed to clear. To the left, a man was playing a flute in a beautiful soft tune that he could barely hear; he listened to that, picking out each note and separating it from the voices that surrounded them.

He traced his fingers around Beth's smooth skin and as he listened to the music, he felt himself return to normal.

Beth looked into his dark eyes, which had returned to normal and shone in the light, and said, "Try to keep him out; he's trying to fuck with us."

The fact that this entity had somehow entered his mind almost made his skin crawl.

"Is he near?" he asked her.

She nodded, "He can hear us."

He focused on her and he saw her moist eyes momentarily give away the fear in her heart. The crowd marched on oblivious to the danger that lay deep within the celebrations, building up for the main show at 7:00pm; it was now 6:34.

Chapter Twenty-Three

Looming

Freya watched as the tall figure sat on the furthest log from the fire, enveloped in a woollen grey shawl. Her long black hair shone wetly in the sun, as Ulla drank her broth. She had been sitting in the same place for hours, accepting drinks from those around her, who were concerned, but never acknowledging them.

So far, she had not uttered a word to anyone. She was weak and her eyes focused on a spot in the distance. Never did she look at Freya, who had been told by the elders of Fahra Point to stay away from the foreigner.

Mahrie, one of the elders who had been watching Ulla carefully, quietly sat down beside Freya. The old woman passed her a mug of hot chocolate, which Freya was thankful for.

Mahrie had noticed her watching the mysterious arrival as if she were some sort of white witch that she dare not touch or come close to. The reason for the witch's arrival was unknown, but what she had done for the settlement spoke better than any words she could utter to them, at least for now.

Mahrie said, "She's beautiful, is she not? How did a lass like that just come out of thin air? That's what I want to know."

Freya replied, "I wish I knew why she was here."

"She might not be here for a reason, love. Sometimes in their own journeys, people just lose their way," Mahrie reasoned, knowing there was probably no coincidence that Ulla had come to defend them from the terrible beasts that had almost destroyed their colony.

Freya considered her point carefully. Perhaps she was right, Ulla had just lost her way and needed comfort. There was something about the woman that meant Freya could not take her eyes off the vision that sat there, absently taking small sips from a can now and then, hands feebly wrapped around the warmth of the container.

"I know you're thinking about your brothers," continued Mahrie, "But don't look so sad; they'll be back before you know it."

Her brothers. She had so far ignored the danger they had put themselves in, preferring to think about the stranger that had saved their lives. She wished she knew what it was, the feeling that grew deep down inside her chest. With a little bit of effort, she managed to force a smile.

Sam had recklessly managed to knock down the bomb, ignoring the protests of Vincent and Timmon. Carefully he kneeled over it, trying to figure out how to stop the mechanism. Vincent had never seen him so angry. He tried to convince Sam to give up, but for the past fifteen minutes he'd been trying to work out how to de-activate the mechanism, sweat building up on his temples.

"Look. It's no good," said Timmon, "The place is going to blow up. We have to get up there and get everybody out!"

"He's right. Listen to him!" shouted Vincent.

Sam turned angrily to Timmon and growled, "Why did you do this?"

"We… thought it would be best for everybody to get the underground back to the way it was, so we could take more control, okay? And once we got involved, we didn't really have a choice any more. He made us do this!" Timmon replied.

"You mean he had some sort of control over you?" Vincent responded, curious but still desperate to get out to the shaft and away from the bombs. He realised if they went off, thousands of people could be hurt or killed.

"Yes, something like that. I don't know. He fucks with your mind. He's here to cause destruction to get something that's important to him but God knows what that something is. I know that he's set up some kind of team at the Aime building because we had to dispose of the bodies."

Sam sighed, looked up and said, "Okay, we have to warn everybody. Try to get them out."

"I'm already going," Vincent replied as he crawled back through the shaft to get to the main floor. His movements echoed down the shaft in front of them.

Timmon decided to go down the chute to warn the residents below while Sam followed Vincent to the top.

Quickly the two brothers climbed the rungs of the fire escape, preparing for the pandemonium that was about to ensue.

Xanther and Beth could now see the main stage; it loomed brightly in the centre of the main underground level. Whatever show was rumoured to be performed here at 7 pm had already worked up a crowd as some people jumped up to touch the wooden stage and others were selling drinks up ahead.

They had seen no leaflets for the performance that was due to start and judging from the voices around them the show had spread merely from word of mouth. It seemed bigger than any street performance that had been shown earlier.

Beth instantly felt a sense of unease building up inside her, as she noticed the attention it was bringing amongst the crowd. She sensed he was near but also something worse; something sinister was about to happen.

She let go of Xanther's hand and stepped forward quickly, past the main stage and through the masses of people, searching every face for his face. She didn't even know what he looked like, but somehow deep down she knew.

It was then he stood out to her. How she knew didn't matter. His pale face stood out in the crowd, unmoving, the only face perfectly still staring straight forward at her.

Things around her seemed to speed up, the people moving faster into a blur while she felt suspended in the same spot; she stared with horror at his still face.

He started to walk closer towards her, gradually speeding up to the same pace as the people surrounding them, bitter intent almost etched into his features. His eyes seemed to cruelly penetrate her soul.

Hands grabbed her from behind and she let out a scream, barely audible with all the background noise. She struggled, almost falling to the ground as Xanther tried to help her to steady herself.

She turned wildly to see him looking scared; his hand gently gripped her arm. Confused, she mouthed the words *get out*, before brushing his arm off her. Turning to face him once more, things seemed to move in slow motion. Beth's face was a deathly pale that almost matched his, and Xanther froze when he saw him.

It was as if his heart turned to ice and all the blood in his body had come to a standstill.

Billy stood before them, his smile widening across his face. Xanther could just tell there was something inhuman about him as he reached out as if to touch Beth. She jumped back in alarm.

"Something wrong, children?" He turned to Beth. Sighing in pleasure he continued, "Beth, I knew you'd come."

Anger and rage somehow flushed into her system. Shaking she shouted, "Who are you? You must leave this place!"

"You know who I am and what I am. I'm not leaving without you," he replied, his voice calm but cold and cruel.

Xanther felt for her hand, as she shouted, "I'll never leave here, this is my home now! You have to stop what's happening; this world is not yours to destroy."

"You brought it on yourself, 'Beth'. You never thought they'd actually let you go, did you?" he told her, sounding disgusted at the sound of her name.

His expression suddenly changed to delight as he added, "Let's see how much you like this place when the time's up and all the rules change!"

"No!" she was screaming at him, her body shaking violently as Xanther tried to hold her back from him, trying to keep her safe.

Billy laughed at her feeble attempts to attack him, her skinny arms held back by her boyfriend, who looked equally weak.

For a second he looked distracted, his eyes focusing on some far away point before returning back to the moment.

"Oh," he said, "It's almost time. You know where I'll be." He looked at her confused expression, and then smiled.

"Can't you feel it? I know you can," he told her.

He started to walk into the crowd, something disappearing into a blur and then gone.

Xanther pulled Beth round to look at him, "What did he mean by that, Beth?" But she seemed to be in some sort of trance. He shook her, and she focused on his eyes as if awakening from a dream.

"Erm, I don't know! I can feel something... I don't..." They were interrupted by Sam and Vincent running through the crowd. They were shouting something, Xanther made out the word 'bomb' from their lips.

Their screams soon became audible to the couple, who stood still as many around them began to move quickly towards the North Gate. A lot of the revellers looked scared and confused, while others carried on oblivious with the celebrations.

They heard Vincent shouting, "Get out, the place is rigged with bombs and it's about to blow up!" A cold sense of dread entered Xanther's body as he watched them running towards them. The old alarms started to sound through the building as people trampled over each other to reach the exits. It was five minutes to seven.

Deep within the panic in the heart of the underground, Kordian struggled to open the grate that kept the residents on the lower level. All the doors seemed to be locked and people were panicking in the fire shaft, trying to push through to the main level.

The lights had dimmed and around them, many rushed through the tunnels and walkways trying to get to the main gates.

The elevators leading to the lower levels had ceased to work, leaving people trapped inside trying to reach the top.

Not knowing how much time they had left, Kordian pulled hard on the grate as he was joined by others trying to help the many people trapped beneath. They were shouting and banging on the wall, demanding to be let out of their prison.

"Hold on," he shouted down to them. "If you move back we'll try and open it!"

They didn't comply, desperate to open the grate as the four men pulled hard in a bid to detach it from the opening of the shaft.

Suddenly the grate did break, sending Kordian and the others backwards into the ground as people pulled themselves up onto the main level, many others climbing the rungs beneath them.

Xanther felt like an outsider, not really there as Beth soon jumped in to help with the evacuation, guiding people to the exits and generally kicking up a fuss to make people take notice.

He woke himself up and joined in with the others, as thousands of people fled the underground. It was then he noticed Beth's face change. She became very agitated and scared. She started to run south, and all he could do was call her name as he watched her begin to disappear into the crowd of faces around her.

Thankfully she turned and shouted to him, "I've got to help Uncle! Meet me outside!" His heart sank further, as the Red was near the South Gate entrance while they were at the North. Then she was gone, and he was left alone.

The alarms rang through his ears loudly, the tones seemed to blend into one as he looked around at the crowd which didn't seem to be diminishing. He knew something was definitely wrong as people shouted cries to open the gates. He didn't understand why the gates would have locked, as he ran through the block of people that had gathered, filling up the gate walkway.

He saw that the gate was indeed closed, while Daire and one of the guards were trying desperately to open it. Some of the crowd were also trying to help get the gate open, while others were becoming very agitated.

"Fuck," he muttered under his breath, before pushing up the ramp towards the gate to the annoyance of many.

Daire spotted him running towards them, and shouted, "I can't open it! It's way too strong – like it's jammed!"

Xanther punched the wall in exasperation. Time was running out unless they could somehow open the gates. The heat was starting to get to him, making the sweat run down his forehead.

He noticed the guard; he looked in his mid-thirties, but in good shape and dressed in a black top, waistcoat and black leather trousers.

Xanther felt a surge of energy flash through him. He asked the guard, "Have you tried the manual override code?"

The guard looked dumbstruck, before issuing his response.

"Look, buddy, we haven't had the need to use that for a long time. I'm only here because of the festival, I…we don't get told that."

"I can't fucking believe they wouldn't tell you something so important," Xanther sighed, as he tried to resurrect an old memory buried deep inside.

He took a deep breath, before saying, "I know something that might not work, but I guess we've got nothing to lose."

"What, what?" The guard exclaimed, but Xanther had momentarily gone somewhere else. A look of concentration crossed his face as he searched his mind through painful memories. The short memory flashed in his eyes.

It had been many years ago when he was a young boy of fifteen lured into the rebellion. He'd gathered in a small, dirty room with Andrew at his side when it was first decided they'd storm the underground together. They were in for a fight; winning would lead to the ultimate territory of the underground.

Loaded with weapons they'd found a weak link in the system, the secondary manual override code only to be used in the most absolute emergency. It was a cheat, a simple cheat to the system.

They had been young and taken advantage of, they hadn't realised that by going in first they'd be the first to fall. Andrew had shown him the code, a seven letter sequence and together they'd opened the gates. They found themselves slipping inside before anyone knew of the threat.

But Andrew had been reckless, ready to fight and ready to die. Xanther saw him shoot down the first guard and then

Andrew was on the floor, his blood seeping onto the hard concrete and his screams, the screams of little more than a child filled the room.

The rest of the 'squad' soon joined while Xanther watched from his hiding place, terrified to move. Many died that day, and many fights were fought soon after until one day the gangs came to a truce and the underground became what it is today.

Now with the alarms sounding around him and the lives of thousands depending on him, he remembered the code that had been forgotten in his mind for so long.

He also knew that he only had one chance; if the code was entered incorrectly the whole system would shut down and reset.

He opened the side-panel and shakily typed in the numbers, zoning out all the sounds, screams and panic around him. The numbers lit blue every time he touched them, until all seven numbers were lit. For a second the alarms stopped and his whole body went tense.

Daire was staring at the door, his heart in his mouth as he saw the thinnest crack appear in the gate, widening until it was open and people pushed past to clamber out of the steel doors.

Xanther stood smiling and emotionally exhausted, watching the crowd running out into the cool evening air. The air seemed to revitalise his hot skin, making everything feel fresh for a further few seconds.

Beth had found Uncle trying to guide his nephews out to the gate but when she saw the crowd in front, unmoving and panicking her heart fell. She understood at once that the gate wouldn't open and she felt terrified for everyone around her. Most of all, she felt pain at leaving Xanther behind at the North Gate.

One of the young nephews clung to her hip and she picked him up, holding him tight against her as she cried.

They were in no way at the front of the crowd, but she could see people banging on the gate anxiously and screaming. The alarms were still going off loudly until suddenly there was a short break in the rhythm and she noticed a slither of blackness in the gate. She watched as people began to filter out, and keeping hold of the boy she helped Uncle towards the ramp.

People were pushing past them violently, desperate to leave the underground system. Someone had pushed the old man over, and frantically she pushed her way back to help him stand. He looked so old to her at that moment, like he had little time left.

Everything went black as the explosions ricocheted through the underpasses and walkways like a black wave of death.

Many were violently blown through the gates and into the streets above by the force of the bombs. Beth was thrown far into a pile-up of people who had all been running for their lives, many of them crushed against the walls at either side of the gate. Others were blown far away from the underground opening onto the streets outside, the blasts causing extensive damage to the area around the gates.

Kordian found himself surrounded by thick heavy smoke, the explosions still ringing in his ears. He coughed as the smoke filled his lungs and he looked around trying to focus on anything solid around him.

He saw others looking shocked and confused; ahead of him it sounded like the streets above had collapsed, blocking the way.

It was quite dark around him and he couldn't quite make out many of the shapes he saw before him, the smoke doing little to help the situation.

He couldn't really tell if anyone had been injured around him as he struggled to breathe in fresh air. Many people covered their mouths with pieces of clothing and their faces which he could barely see looked dirty from the explosions.

A man was shouting something, but he couldn't hear a word of it, his ears ringing from the blasts. Others stumbled towards one of the gates, Kordian couldn't remember which one anymore. He realised they probably weren't safe.

Standing up he moved his arms, shouting, "Stop, don't go any further! The ground probably isn't stable!"

He was ignored. Only some of the survivors stayed to look after those who were still in shock. A girl was shaking on the floor, terrified to move, while an older man stroked her hair and spoke words which he guessed were soothing.

Carefully, he started to walk forward through the survivors, looking for anyone that needed his help, telling them to stay where they were.

He didn't want to trigger any more explosions but considering the smoke he guessed that at least one of the bombs had probably malfunctioned or had not gone off properly. Thinking about it, he realised it was probably the latter if the bombs had been assembled by Neil's gang.

A girl grabbed Kordian's hand, leading him to the side and he only just made out her voice asking if he was okay. He nodded, and they sat down together as she rubbed his arm. He felt pain as he noticed it hurt.

He thought of his brothers and wondered if they had got above ground in time to stop the explosions before he began to cough a series of deep, harsh coughs that hurt his chest.

When Beth came to, all she heard was a buzzing noise like she had fallen asleep next to a wasps' nest. Sleepily she acknowledged the buzzing, her body feeling numb she opened her eyes to the horror that surrounded her.

She saw people screaming and injured, bodies lay scattered around and part of the main street had been completely turned over. Huge craters had formed in the ground and some people were covered in mud and blood.

She saw a girl screaming, her hands over her head but Beth could hear no sound, only buzzing. Looking around all she saw was destruction, people still emerging from the underground with lost limbs and others lying dead beside her.

Underneath her she realised, was the corpse of a child. Shakily she pulled herself to her feet having no wish to look at his or her face.

Blood was running down her thigh and she absent-mindedly rubbed it, feeling a slight pain as she walked through the bodies and the injured.

Helplessly, she only thought to look for him, her love. Ridiculously, all she could see was death and pain around her. It seemed to go on forever, taunting her.

She walked on numbly, until the pain in her heart began to filter through and she let out one sob, then two. She screamed but it was like she was hearing herself through cotton wool.

Figures were walking around her; she ignored them as she kept moving towards the direction of North Gate, somehow taking care not to step on those spread out on the ground. Tears ran down her dirty face, a single red scar on her forehead marking her maybe forever. She didn't care about herself, she didn't care about walking anymore but somehow she kept going, the realisation sinking deeper into her heart.

She noticed she'd reached the North Gate site, but looking around she saw nothing she recognised.

"Where are you…" she whispered, her eyes scanning the ground and the injured. There looked to be nothing left, the people standing bore no resemblance to Xanther.

Frantically she started to search the bodies, her breath getting heavier and heavier and her heart pounded as she expected to see him lying there, dead, on the ground.

As she snapped out of it, she looked up at the huge hole in the ground that seemed to lead on towards hell. She could see movement.

Out of the smoke came two barely visible figures walking towards her. Looking closely, she noticed one was holding the other up, and she knew then that he had come back to her.

Somehow, she found the strength to run towards them. Daire looking slightly worse for wear as he supported Xanther.

Tears streaming down her eyes she leapt up to them both, hugging them and screaming emotionally, "I thought you were dead!"

"Not yet," said Xanther, before collapsing in Beth's arms as the sobs ripped through her, taking hold of her completely.

She fell to the ground, holding him and crying for those who had lost their lives. Daire was looking around for his brothers but unable to leave her side. Xanther's mind filled with something ridiculous and utterly pointless from the past.

It was a fine day in spring, on the day of the crow. He was young then, surrounded by friends. It was Kristin's garden and as they had called on Xanther earlier, he had joined in on the fun and was now with them discussing what kind of game they could play.

He was with Kristin, a year younger than himself, Jack who was the same age and Samantha who was only seven. He was nine years of age, his young face covered in freckles.

The sun began to shine down through the clouds. It was a boring time and the children decided to go and look for something to do. They hadn't been looking for anything in particular, but they did find more than they had prepared for.

They began to watch through the rows of hedges, over the lawn and onto the patio. Xanther was looking for ladybirds. He'd always loved ladybirds.

He had already seen some young ones about, as it was a particularly warm spring. He didn't know what the others were looking for, but they laughed and joked all the same. They had spent many a happy time in that garden, but Kristin's mother demanded quietness from them as she used to work the nightshift as a nurse. Because of this there was a general air of edginess in the atmosphere.

It was Jack who was the noisiest among them. Xanther was so shy he could hardly speak to adults sometimes. The last thing he wanted to do was anger Kristin's parents. Jack started shouting, taunting and jumping around the garden. He could never really take a hint, and they all looked at her in shock. Idiotic taunts about his boredom began to blast in sound waves above Kristin's mother's bedroom. The front door slammed shut soon after.

"What the hell! Mum's trying to sleep!" shouted Neil, Kristin's older brother. Xanther got the shivers; he didn't like being told off by anyone and Jack stopped dead in his tracks. His face fell, and in his mind Xanther wanted to retreat away from this older boy.

Slamming the door shut behind him, he was gone again, can of juice in hand. Xanther looked at the others, and suggested they go back around the garden again. It was in the hedges that they found it: a crow, lying there, helpless. It looked either paralysed or dead, and he watched as Jack and Kristin pushed Samantha away and examined it.

"It's got a heartbeat!" Kristin said, finger on its chest. He felt saddened, he didn't like to see weak animals and this one was obviously not moving or trying to escape. He could see it now, its black feathers shining in the sun. It certainly looked very ill. Jack was stroking its wings; Kristin was still listening to its heart.

"We should maybe take it to a vet," Kristin said, looking worried. He decided to get closer to take a look, so he pushed her out of the way. It's funny how when you are younger you always want everything for yourself.

"Let me see," Xanther said. He put his finger where its heart was, and could feel something. But at the same time, a very bad feeling came over him. The bird's eye was missing and as he stared into its eye socket, he saw a glimmer of movement before he realised with a sudden shock that this bird was dead. Dead and filled with maggots.

He screamed; he had to. Everyone crouched over, wanted to know what it had done and he just wanted to get away from this dead thing. The maggots had taken over its body and although the bird was dead, it was filled with life. He screamed because he found this thing absolutely horrifying, wanted to get away from that moment and everything around him. He was making loud noises and Kristin's mother wouldn't be pleased but none of that mattered anymore.

That life goes on was a valuable lesson for him. And when he looked back, amongst that dead corpse and the little wriggly things that were eating it, he realised that nothing looks that bad really.

He woke up surrounded by death and started to laugh hysterically as Beth looked at him, confused.

Xanther squeezed her hand, his dark eyes opened wide as she looked down at him knowing that at least he was not lost to her. Somehow it didn't seem to matter that the amount of pain hurt her in ways she couldn't even begin to imagine.

He was in pain too, but his beautiful eyes were dry as he looked up at her calmly, as if she was all that mattered in the mess around them.

His head hurt and people were screaming around them, completing the chaos.

Chapter Twenty-Four

Her Power

Night had fallen at Fahra Point, and loneliness had long occupied Freya's mind. She had seen no sign of Lucian all day and she wondered if the old man had left the settlement entirely.

She had felt completely alone, the outsider child, as the settlers milled around all day, completing tasks and preparing meals. She had watched Ulla carefully, her blank eyes staring at what seemed to be nothing.

For some reason, Freya felt a strange connection with the woman as she sat there. She knew in a way they were both outsiders, but whatever secrets the stranger kept were locked deep inside her, at least for now.

She was supposed to be in bed, as old-fashioned Mahrie had set up her bed for the night and given her a glass of milk to help her sleep. It seemed like they wanted to keep her far away from them, as if she was the one that had brought on Jared's death; the city child far from home. She could never feel at home here, although they probably did not mean to treat her so coldly.

Her bed was small, with woven blankets piled high and one thin pillow that looked worn out. It was snug but Freya had no inclination to find her dreams so early.

Instead, she found herself cautiously placing her feet onto the cold grass as she climbed out of the wagon. Looking around the settlement, she could see no one. The fire's last burning embers still glowed in the dark.

She could hear two voices further away in the forest, laughing and joking, probably drunk on beer. Moving swiftly away from the sounds she headed for Lucian's tent.

The wind whispered gently around her, almost like voices chilling her to the bone. Goose bumps stood out on her arm as she ran the rest of the way towards the newest canvas tent, set up by Lucian himself.

No light came from inside as she silently opened the door and looked in. There was no movement visible to her and she knew it to be empty. She felt a shiver down her spine that somehow urged her to go inside the tent. She felt exposed outside in the camp as if something icy and cold were to jump up behind her and freeze her blood.

The tent was eerily silent and she realised the floor was lined with different fabrics. Her foot touched something cold as she reached the middle of the floor. It glinted at her and she realised it was a candle holder; they'd been set out, though unlit in a circle in the middle of the room.

A small dresser stood to the right of the room and something that lay on top of it caught her eye from across the tent. She walked towards it as it glowed in the darkness and she reached out to pick it up.

It was some kind of stone attached to a long chain. She held the chain up, examining it. It seemed to glow brighter and then back to normal in her hand.

A noise came from outside the tent, and at once she knew it was Lucian. Quickly she hid behind the dresser with the stone still clutched in her hand.

She saw his tall frame enter the tent and he whispered under his breath, something that she couldn't quite understand. He seemed to stand still for quite a while before moving forward and kneeling down to pick up the candle which had fallen. She couldn't make out his eyes.

His long robes hung down almost to his feet, his sandals barely visible in the darkness. His hair was not tied back as usual but instead had been left to hang.

Lucian was now in the middle of the circle, still holding the fallen candle in his hand, lifting it to eye level. He seemed to motion with something in his other hand and somehow made the candle alight. It burned a bright yellow in the darkness and Freya could now make out some of the features on his wrinkled, worn face.

He used the candle to light the others around the circle, whispering a chant in some sort of strange language. She listened closely as the chanting seemed to get faster, but she could not understand what he was saying or why. The chanting relaxed her as she watched him kneel down in the circle that he had created around him. She could see his robes were bright blue as they shone under the candlelight.

Freya could hear rain starting to fall outside, hitting off the thick white canvas behind her in small taps like tiny feet.

His chanting stopped abruptly and for a second she was convinced he knew where she was, had spotted her hiding place. Her heart almost stopped in her chest as his head turned towards the cabinet; he seemed to be looking at the space where the necklace had been and she realised she still had the chain delicately wrapped around her hand.

Before he could register what had happened, the tent door seemed to fly open making him turn quickly. He jumped up and stood in the circle of candles watching the empty doorway. The rain had increased and he moved swiftly to slam the door shut.

The circle he'd created had been momentarily broken and as he stepped back into it he noticed the dark figure that occupied the corner of the tent. Lucian jumped back in surprise and then Freya saw it too; she recognised the tall figure with the long dark hair.

Ulla slowly stepped forward like darkness taking over the room.

"Lucian," she spoke in hushed but dark and foreign tones that Freya could not place, "Isn't it a little dangerous to be playing with flames in your current situation?"

He seemed to take a deep breath, as if consigned to whatever would happen next.

"And pray tell, what might that be?" he asked, her eyes flashing purple under the candlelight. She looked even more alien, Freya thought, as the rain poured down outside. She heard thunder in the background as she tried to curl into a tighter ball behind the dresser.

Ulla's voice sounded like cruel velvet as she spoke, "You knew I'd come, didn't you?"

Lucian nodded as she continued, "And you knew I would not let you get away with what you did to me in the forest? A simple disablement spell, indeed."

"It was all I could think of to numb you, Ulla. You have no place here and no right to intrude on these people."

Ulla cut in, "Do you have any idea how long I lay in that forest for, listening to the sounds of the earth! It was only a matter of time before I called for you Lucian."

"Maybe," Lucian replied, "But I allowed you to come, did I not? I am prepared for what happens next."

Ulla's face contorted into a smile, as she moved forward towards the old man. Her long grey dress made of see-through mesh dragged along the ground; the settlers had been unable to remove the dress and instead covered her with a shawl for warmth.

Now Freya saw she was not just half a woman anymore, a beautiful empty shell with no spirit instead. She was very much alive, her spirit lighting up her purple eyes and turning the air almost electric.

Her arms reached out to Lucian as he grimaced back in the circle, Freya watching terrified from behind him. She sensed Ulla was about to do something awful to Lucian as she walked straight through one of the candles, her dress momentarily catching the flame before it blackly fizzled out.

Lucian was chanting something under his breath as she approached him and suddenly he screamed out as if in terrible pain. He turned in desperation towards the cabinet and seemed to reach out to where the stone had once glowed and saw it empty.

The stone seemed to get very hot in her hand, and she knew at once she had to do something.

Holding the stone high she stood up in view of Ulla, and shouted, "Leave Lucian alone. Go back to where you came from!"

Lucian turned to the young girl in horror as he noticed she held the emblem in her hand. The fact that she could even hold it astonished him and with desperation he realised she could harness its power.

"Freya, the emblem! Use it. Direct the force at her!"

Ulla laughed, the sound unpleasant to Freya's ears, "Why, little girl, I thought you would want to help the pretty lady."

She overpowered Lucian with her force, brightly flashing from her aura imprisoning him and making him gasp in harsh breaths.

Ulla seemed to hold Lucian in her energy force as the stone felt suddenly heavier in Freya's hand, almost becoming alive with power. It violently shook in her hand and a blue and green light seemed to flash again and again. Ulla screamed in pain, making Freya feel dizzy and light.

Lucian looked as vulnerable as a child as Ulla's power seemed to overtake the whole room, contradicting the force of the stone. She started to rise, taking Lucian with her and the tent seemed to come apart from the top.

Heavy canvas material fell over Freya and she dropped the stone as she helplessly watched Ulla rise with Lucian into the cold air, the force that joined them seeming to become even stronger.

Freya realised that during the time at the settlement, instead of being drained of energy, Ulla had simply been channelling it, saving it for this moment. It occurred to her that Lucian had known this, had been aware of it since her arrival at the settlement. He had failed to stop her and now she had come to claim him.

A sudden flash of lightning struck the pair and they vanished completely into the night sky, the light seeming to pull them into another world.

"No!" shouted Freya as she searched the sky for a sign of Lucian, any sign of light. She saw nothing apart from darkness, vaguely aware of the settlers crowding around her, touching her head and shaking body.

She felt strangely numb as she looked at the stone lying on the grass. Dead of any energy it looked dull and faded. She picked it up and put it in her pocket before Mahrie wrapped her in a warm blanket and lifted her somewhere warm.

The settlers were talking amongst themselves, looking into the sky where their betrayer had vanished.

She felt Ulla's presence for a while after she was gone, whether in her mind or the air around her. Shivering she fell asleep that night on Mahrie's chest as one last thought entered her mind, echoing through her subconscious: *I could have saved him.*

Chapter Twenty-Five

The Journey

Xanther savoured the cool rain upon his face, cooling his skin. He and Beth had been working for hours helping the many injured from the huge explosion. People were still trapped underground and some of the brothers were helping out with the emergency services to try and free them.

Many lay dead around them still. Xanther had gotten used to the carnage that surrounded them.

It had been particularly bad on Beth, as she blamed herself for most of what had happened. Although she hadn't really spoken about it, he could tell that she was heartbroken.

Her hair was a knotted mess, her dress dirty and ripped and her boots falling to pieces as she worked to help those still in need of attention.

Xanther approached her, pulling her to the side and grabbing her attention almost selfishly.

"You look exhausted, Beth. You need to stop now," he told her gently, his arm touching her bare shoulder.

"I know… they'll get the help they need but I feel so fucking responsible." He looked into her eyes; the seemingly non-stop tears that had washed her face clean meant that she could cry no more. She looked weak and broken.

Although barely a scratch showed on her slender body she walked as if a weight had been hung around her neck, pulling her down.

Sam had a broken leg and sat at the edge of the scene, his leg covered in bandages. A small fire burned. He had refused a journey to the hospital, wishing to stay with his brothers.

Daire and Vincent had put all their energy into helping the fire services and first aid teams although it was still considered very dangerous to reach the underground areas. The ground was very unstable and could easily collapse even more, possibly killing more of the people trapped underneath.

Vincent, a few scratches more the wiser was convinced Kordian was trapped somewhere under the rubble, Daire had to physically stop him from going underground himself to search.

It was very late when they decided to stop and rest. Sam had prepared a simple meal with some supplies from the emergency teams and it was handed out among the survivors before they sat down to eat themselves.

Beth had looked subdued for some time, and Xanther watched her now slowly chewing on her food. When she finally spoke, he was not surprised by what she had to say.

"I need to leave here. I know where to find him," she said, momentarily catching everyone's attention. She looked deadly serious.

"Where is he?" Xanther asked.

"It doesn't matter." She shook her head, "But I have to get there before it's too late."

Sam and the others looked confused, "Wait a minute, who is he?"

Xanther replied, "He's one of the Chaka, a sort of messenger. He appeared just before you warned us of the explosions; he had a message for Beth." He didn't trust Billy one little bit.

Sam looked at both of them, trying to work out the meaning of what Xanther had said. He asked, "Why did he have a message for Beth?"

"Because that's not the full story," Beth replied before Xanther could intervene, "He came here for me. You see... I'm one of them, but I don't want to be. I feel like everything is my fault and I have to put an end to it, once and for all."

Everyone was quiet as the moments seemed to pass by, Sam looked down at his hands and Vincent looked utterly shocked.

"I'm s-sorry," she stuttered as Xanther pulled her close to him.

Vincent looked about to say something, but Sam muttered, "Why the hell didn't you tell us before? Look, I left my little girl behind at that settlement...if I lose her I don't know what I'll do with myself. If you can stop this, Beth, I'll trust you to stop it. I just want this place safe again for Freya."

Xanther could never have imagined the truth; that Sam was Freya's dad had never even crossed his mind.

Beth said, "I was scared. You don't know what it's like to be chased for the rest of your life. They never let me go. I thought it was safe here."

"You're not human, are you?" Vincent asked her. Beth shook her head slowly.

She remembered what it had been like to be chased in that car with her sisters, when the car had fallen and she thought she'd lost Tristan forever. The smell of burning tyres and water filled her lungs as she'd been pulled out of the sea by Emma, her sister.

She could still feel the pain, the terrible loss of her sisters and the overwhelming sense of happiness when she was reunited with Tristan one last time. She had thought then that everything had been worth it, to have her love and to live together in Middletown as brother and sister.

Her heart had finally seemed to self destruct after what happened to Tristan, and no amount of pain and fear could penetrate her mind again, her heart dead in her chest. She kept on living for the sake of living, blocking out any thoughts that they, the Chaka might be coming for her once again.

All she wanted was to escape from the horror of their world, the pain and destruction they caused and the overwhelming greed to consume everything that wasn't already dead.

Sam's voice broke her thoughts, "Beth, are you sure you want to do this?"

"They need to be stopped or they will consume everything in this world too. I know how to quell their darkness and this is something I have to do alone." They seemed to consider this.

"I can't leave my daughter...she doesn't even know the truth," Sam sighed, accepting that she must fight the final battle without his help.

"No," Xanther said, "I'm not letting you go alone. If you have to do this, I'm coming with you."

The group spoke for a long time about Beth's journey, the pain she'd felt and the terrible anguish she'd dealt with for so many years until finally, they began to understand that she must go and face the Chaka once and for all.

They remembered the good times they had shared and Xanther realised that this journey had been the most worthwhile of his life. The rest seemed empty and dull; he could not imagine staying in Middletown without Beth.

As midnight approached, they helped Beth prepare for the journey ahead of her and Xanther. Together they looked strong, Beth's heart most definitely alive with anger, pain and yes, love. Love for Xanther, for Sam and his brothers and for Orenia.

As the couple left the destruction of the underground and headed off into the darkness of the streets, Beth knew deep down in her heart that he was waiting with bated breath. His presence would not leave her thoughts, making her shiver at Xanther's side. She felt fear for him that she kept deep inside her.

Chapter Twenty-Six

Tristan

As they walked into the darkness to begin the short journey that lay ahead of them, Beth began her own personal journey. She squeezed Xanther's hand; he seemed strong despite all the madness around them. She didn't understand how he could love her still, her no matter what problems she had caused in his home town. He knew he loved her with everything he had left to love.

She realised she had buried the pain inside her for long enough. Now she had to come to terms with what had happened before she made her final stand. The darkness seemed to pull them forward, towards the sick creature that lay in wait.

Xanther meant more to her than she could ever have imagined possible, He was the other half of her life. But she was plagued by thoughts of what she had done as the terrifying truth set into her mind. The Chaka had returned and they had found her.

Memories of Tristan flooded her mind as she remembered what had happened on the day that had changed everything, the day she first knew in a way that they had come back into her life.

His curly golden brown hair shone in the sun as he smiled at her, green eyes staring deep into hers. She had loved him with all her heart back then, lovingly grasping the time they spent together as if she knew somehow that time would be short.

It had been like the world stopped when she saw him again for the first time; nothing could have prepared her for the love that flooded back and although she couldn't understand how he was still alive she accepted it without thinking.

They had embraced like nothing else in the world mattered to them, and together they set up their own little nest.

Every day she woke up to see his angelic face and messed up hair and she felt truly happy, as if a miracle had somehow found her when she never imagined it could.

They had lived together happily as she went to her job as a waitress and he worked in the underground. Every day she spent with Tristan felt like a gift that had been given to her.

Looking back she could see the cracks; never once did they talk about what had happened to him after the accident. At the time she would have swore he had died as there was no sign of him in the water. She used to dream that he'd survived, that they had escaped together. Always in her dreams he was alive in the old house, holding her hands beside the boarded-up windows.

But she had searched the sea for him until she could no longer wait and her sisters had needed her. Together they escaped, leaving the remains of the car behind, terrified for their lives.

After she thought she had lost everything to start afresh in Middletown, she found him in the place she least expected. She couldn't question, she couldn't violate the moment, all she could do was surrender to it.

Now she knew that she had been so stupid and naïve to think that everything would be the same between them. On the surface, he was the same Tristan, but subconsciously she could not trust the fact that he had been there waiting.

Lying in bed with him those first few days had been heaven. It was like they could finally be a proper couple. Apart from the few friends she'd made in the underground, he was all she had left.

To their friends, they became brother and sister, Beth and Luke. They were happy and spent most of their time together. They made love just like they always had, had conversations in the same way but their past was something they ignored. Not once did they bring up the Chaka and the world they'd fled long ago. Beth was happy that way and never questioned it.

Then it began; some nights he seemed to go very cold. Not physically but emotionally cold as if something wasn't right between them. It was then she started to wonder where he'd been, as if he'd been somewhere to make him act so differently.

On those nights she would try to talk to him, to touch him and he wouldn't respond to her, brushing her away and not eating the meals she had prepared for them both.

One night, when he was in this sort of phase, she approached him cautiously. She asked him, "Do you think the Chaka are affecting you?"

"No, I don't," he replied, his voice low and unchanging, almost icy. Stepping back she felt a coldness in her heart as she sat on their bed, one small tear ran down her left cheek.

The weeks went by as winter fell. Every so often she'd be sitting typing on her computer when she would look up to see him standing there, staring at her. He seemed to do this silently, and what scared her was that at those times he didn't seem like the same Tristan.

Sometimes she tried to smile at him but he was unresponsive, as if coming out of some deep trance. He'd snap out of it, as if he didn't realise how he'd even got there.

Beth would lie awake some nights as he lay sleeping next to her, just thinking about where they had come from. It chilled her to her very soul to imagine anything changing him, to imagine that they could have found her after everything she'd been through to get to where she was. She'd built a home that she could finally rest in and did not want to lose the love she thought she'd lost.

One day she had returned home from her job. It was late afternoon and the sun was out yet the air frosty around her. She was remembering the strange feeling she got when she noticed the feathers scattered across the grass in front of the house.

She dismissed the feeling, thinking it had probably been a cat as she retrieved the door key from her pocket. But as she got nearer the door she realised it had been left ajar.

A couple of feathers lay on the stairs and the sound of silence filled the house, making the feeling of unease return.

Tristan had left his gun on the hall table, unusual as he'd always been so careful to store it in the past, especially when they had lived in the underground.

Carefully she lifted the gun and checked the safety catch, the corner of her eyes checking that the living room was clear. She would normally have called his name but something stopped her from doing do.

Quietly she had climbed the stairs, gun in her hand as she entered the top hallway. She registered the noise; a soft slightly wet sound that she couldn't quite place.

The bedroom door was ever so slightly open; she rested her hand on the door and gently pushed.

He was sitting on the bed with his back to her, feathers scattered the floor. He had something in his hand that she could only guess to be the missing bird. From his movements it looked like he was ravenously eating it like an animal that'd just caught its prey.

She was unable to hold back a low moan as she started to tremble in the doorway. His body seemed to snap to attention and quickly his head turned to face the door. Only it wasn't his face anymore.

His mouth was covered in blood and feathers, his bloodshot eyes focused on her manically as he dropped the dead bird. He seemed to lunge off the bed towards her, making an animalistic noise which made her skin crawl.

He jumped on her and she hit him with the gun as he bit her clothes. She screamed and kicked but he was too strong. She shot him in the head, trying to get back from him. Bits of his flesh had been blown onto the floor and still he didn't stop coming for her. She shot him again.

He lay on the floor, twitching and all she could do was watch, shaking and pale. Eventually she kicked him hard; until he eventually stopped moving and it was then she broke down, sobbing and screaming in pain as she realised she'd killed her love.

It was a secret she kept hidden from everyone, the pain so deep, it cut a fresh wound every time it entered her mind.

For a while she thought she was going insane, but luckily Sam and the others took her in, looked after her. She had been hysterical when they first arrived, Sam had carried her from the house kicking and sobbing while the others dealt with the mess.

Eventually she'd explained to them that she'd walked in to find him there, dead. She didn't let them know how she'd cleaned up the bird feathers and the carcase before calling them, or how she'd beaten her 'brother' to death.

The guilt stayed in her mind, haunting her dreams and every waking moment, but eventually she returned to work. It kept her busy, helped her hide away the memory and bury it down within herself. But she could never forget, or forgive herself for what she had done.

Chapter Twenty-Seven

The Change

By the time they reached the building it already felt like it was too late. The air all around them seemed to be filled with a sort of electricity that almost seemed alive.

As they approached, the building looked eerily dark and lifeless, the large AIME letters visible in the night sky, as the moon shone down upon the headquarters.

Xanther's dark eyes shone in the light, as he came to a standstill and turned to Beth.

"Are you sure you want to do this?" he asked her.

"I've never been so sure," she replied, and reaching out for his hand, gave it a squeeze before moving forward towards the main entrance.

Xanther was sure of one thing; that 'Billy' was waiting for them. Reaching out to grasp the door handle, he almost felt the electricity shoot through him. But the door was dead, just like the rest of the building. Taking a deep breath and a mutual look, they slowly stepped inside.

As soon as they entered, the lights buzzed and became bright, then flickered dimly, lighting up the hallway leading to reception.

Beth nervously toyed with her blade, her attention leading from one dimly-lit corner to the next, searching for anything out of the ordinary. They listened, only to be met by silence.

The corridor ahead looked less than welcoming, and Xanther shivered as his foot met with the first corpse.

"He killed them all," Beth whispered. Her eyes met with Xanther's and she gestured to move on. He couldn't quite figure out her tone, but it was possibly cold anger. Her eyes almost looked on fire in the light.

She was the strangest being he'd ever met, yet he could never be scared of someone so beautifully in-sync with her own self.

More bodies lay scattered along the corridor as if they'd been running to get away from something. Xanther didn't want to imagine the look on their faces but guessed they were probably filled with terror. His heart beat heavy in his chest and his hands felt shaky.

Beth was steady, like a ninja waiting to pounce and he was almost envious of just how strong she was.

The pair came to the first door, and shakily, Xanther opened it. The room appeared empty. A number of workstations had been set up around the perimeter and a single table lay in the middle. On the table lay one solitary candle, burning brightly. Beth slowly walked through the door, towards the light of the flame. The candle sat on top of what looked like a handkerchief, a hand-sewn 'B' woven into it.

Xanther had followed Beth into the room; her eyes now looked more like flames than ever. She was close-up to the candle now. Her eyes focused on the flame in a way that Xanther found unnerving. The intensity of her gaze seemed only to rise. Whether or not it was his imagination, the room seemed to grow increasingly warmer.

She felt herself slipping into a daze, unable to separate herself from the overwhelming feeling of being somewhere she'd left long ago. It pulled at her heart. The warm feeling spread through her body like water. She started to drift off into a dream, witnessing her body from above; she was vaguely aware something was wrong. Suddenly, she felt a cold ball of ice in the centre of her stomach. Pain and agony swept over her.

"Beth," he whispered, receiving no response.

"Beth… Beth!" He put his hand on her arm, but the heat of her made him jump back. He tried to shake her, and finally something seemed to register in her eyes.

"We need to keep moving. Come on let's get out of here," he said, looking worried. Her head turned slowly, and something about her expression shocked him to the core. A low growl emanated from her throat.

"You follow me here… you know nothing, you fool. Leave here now, the girl belongs to me."

She started to shake and tremble all over, her body seemed to slump and a look of horror crossed over her face and he knew whatever it was had left her. She plunged back into her body as if her soul had known she belonged there. He reached out and held her close to him, a look of panic in his dark eyes.

"Beth? My God, did he take over from the flame?" Xanther asked as her now fragile looking body recovered.

"I-I think he did. Yes. I feel cold all over, so cold…" she replied. He touched her forehead, which was anything but cold.

"I need to get away from that flame," she said, stumbling out of the room, before crouching on the floor, breathing deep and fast, gathering her thoughts.

It was as if everything she'd been through in the last few years, all her memories had been invaded by this…thing. She knew that he was their messenger and he was evil to the core, rotten.

Xanther kneeled down beside her, trying to calm her. He asked, "Did you see anything, when it happened?"

Slowly, she nodded, "I saw far too much of where I came from… then it felt as if he just threw me out of my own body."

He sucked in his breath and sat in silence for a few seconds, biting his lower lip; something he hadn't done since the quarterly exams at university.

"We need to keep moving, okay?" He asked after some time. She nodded and he noticed that her shaking had stopped.

"This guy deserves the biggest piece of me I can give him," she laughed slightly, making him smile even through the current circumstances.

"Look, no matter what happens, I love you and that's never going to change. We'll make it last an eternity. I won't lose you; I won't let that happen Beth."

"What if it already has. It just hasn't sunk in yet?" she spoke, sounding slightly detached but somehow good humoured at the same time. He grabbed her hand and pulled her to her feet.

"I'm afraid you're stuck with me, Miss Pessimistic. Are you ready?"

"Yep," she replied.

She walked alongside Xanther until deep down inside her, she found enough strength to push further forward.

Ahead, a key-card had been jammed in the automatic lock of one of the main doors which remained slightly ajar. It was as if she knew exactly where to go, where to find what they were looking for. Even the puddles of what could only be blood did not slow her down. Xanther admired her spirit which almost seemed to glow from inside her.

The walls seemed to be getting thicker and metal sealed doors now surrounded the inner wall. The electricity seemed to be generating from somewhere within, setting Xanther's nerves even more on edge.

Beth stopped in front of one of the doors, a hint of green light barely showing around it. The fact that it wasn't quite shut meant that it had been left that way for a reason.

He knew exactly what she was going to do next. She walked forward, the door opening for her entrance. The light seemed to almost pull her thin body inside, the thick heavy doors snapping behind her.

"Beth!" Xanther cried out. He didn't have a chance to follow, as if something had grabbed her from inside. Panic rose up inside him as he tried to find a way in. He shouted, "Beth! BETH!"

As the doors snapped shut behind her, she was immersed in a bright colour, a colour that almost hurt her eyes. The room almost felt alive to her, and she struggled to stand upright, feeling dizzy and disorientated.

Nothing felt right in this room, yet at the same time it felt familiar, as if this was the very thing she'd been running from all along.

Out of the silence, a voice spoke.

"Beth," it hissed, as if the taste of the words were too bitter to keep inside, "I've been waiting for you. Your little friend has been locked out, no?"

"Go back to where you came from, you bastard!" All her energy went into her cry.

"If I am going back, then so are you, little one. You can rejoin all your old friends..." Billy laughed, still invisible to Beth through the blinding light which seemed to be focused on one part of the room.

She heard Xanther's voice on the outside, calling her, thumping on the walls and her hatred for Billy grew stronger.

"Shall I kill him now?" The deep voice growled.

"If you do then I'll make sure I kill every single one of your race, messenger boy!" She cried.

"Well then, why don't we bring him inside so he can see just how good your fighting skills really are," Billy replied with the same low growl. His words seemed to blend into each other and she could also hear them within her mind.

One of the doors snapped open and Xanther stumbled inside, blocking his eyes with his hand. Beth called to him, searching for him but seeing nothing.

"What have you done to her?" Xanther shouted.

"The question is more, what am I going to do?" Billy replied, sounding colder and angrier this time.

"Nothing!" Beth screamed, "You're going to do nothing! You've destroyed everything, you fucking murderer!"

A deep, tormented laugh seeped into the room and at once she knew exactly what he was thinking before he began to talk.

"Murderer? Do you mean like you, when you murdered your true love?"

"NO!" Beth screamed.

"Why don't you explain then?" Billy sneered.

"It wasn't him and you know it! He was gone from that body, they turned him into one of them and he tried to kill me!"

"You know why he tried to kill you, love? He was possessed by the *Chaka*, because you had no right to leave and you don't belong in this world! You deserve to rot in your own little hell for eternity and you deserve to know that you killed him when *his soul was still deep down inside*."

Beth screamed out in pain. The words pierced right through her and she fell to the ground. Her memories still haunted her. Tristan, beautiful Tristan had been her protector. She remembered his face when she finally did what she did. A small recognition of her love hit her before she destroyed him for good and sent his soul away. Nothing could ever make her forgive herself for what she had done, and now she knew why.

Anger boiled up inside her. She directed all her hate towards 'Billy' whose evil laughter filled her ears and her mind, overpowering yet refreshing her. She yearned to hear his pain.

He was hiding like a coward. She knew he could hear her thoughts and so she let him, his laughter growing even more intense.

"Ah, little one, you are just as evil as I am." His voice grew clearer. She could sense him closer to her now, yet she was still blind to the light.

"That's our little secret," she replied, a smile forming on her lips.

Xanther tried to follow the sound but as he got near, the light dimmed and a large darkness started to descend on him. Beth sensed Billy's rage, his coldness and anger building up inside. Quickly she threw herself on Xanther, her eyes suddenly focusing on the ancient enemy like a hunter focusing on her prey.

He looked inhuman, his eyes looked dead yet stared deep into her, bore into her soul. His muscles seemed to bulge and grow larger, his teeth sharp and threatening, yet she was no longer scared.

After all the years, the pain and the suffering she had finally stopped running. Her tears had been enough to fill every day with sorrow, yet here he was in front of her, her chance to end her torment. Billy roared out a terrible sound which hurt Xanther's ears, to which Beth was now immune. The horror show seemed surreal as the heat started to build up around the two figures.

The monster, formerly known as Billy, lunged forward and violently tried to push Beth out the way, but the amulet shone, protecting her; it burned and seared through him and looking breakable again. He flew back, the roar turning into the most pitiful howl. She looked down at the amulet shining brightly against the light, as if fuelled by the howling mass of Billy.

"Shut up! You're nothing but a slave, a messenger to open the door for Them! The Chaka don't give a fuck about you. They know I can kill you so easily with this!" She held up the amulet and Billy tried to hide his terror. She used her mind gift to keep him back against the wall before holding on to Xanther, protecting him once more. Billy had seemed to grow weaker, the amulet draining his aura of the power he needed.

Billy's voice rose up, "If they only knew you still had that. You're going to pay, thief!"

"I should finish this now…" she spoke softly, focusing on his eyes that looked far from human in the light of the room.

And then the door did open. The portal was bright with energy now and she sensed them coming forward with such force that it almost hurt to imagine it. She knew what was coming; the spawn of the Chaka. She stepped back, a momentary weakness in her tower of strength.

Billy's rage had now built up so much he had become more than just a solid entity, his energy causing fire to blast in every direction, setting parts of the room alight.

Beth could see the figures coming through the portal, slow and strong, yet they were flesh and bone at the same time. Billy roared and aimed the fire at the portal. The Chaka's spawn were blown through the air and onto the floor. The heat in the room was almost nauseating as the pair struggled to find a way out.

High pitched shrieks could be heard through the fire and many more spawn were still finding their way out of the portal and burning almost immediately, their cries echoing around the room.

Xanther and Beth found themselves running from the backlash, the noise, heat and screams behind them. They left him there, weak and consumed by flames and the barely human clones. The walls seemed almost to be closing in on them, the building watching with a thousand eyes and a voice of pain, Billy's voice still audible far behind them.

They got to the access point and the cool grass just in time to see the thing shoot through the roof. Inhuman its pain seeped into the night air, consumed in flames. It was Billy, only not quite the same Billy.

214

The spawn of the Chaka rose up to reclaim him, pulling him back into the flames, his body too weak to struggle anymore.

Beth collapsed onto the ground holding her hands over her head, his pain audible to her mind with no shut-off point. Xanther joined her. Breathing heavily he held her close to him.

He whispered, "Shit."

The explosion ripped through the building with so much force that they were pushed apart from each other and into the air, far away from the blaze, rendering Xanther unconscious.

Beth whispered to herself three small words, before slowly closing her eyes and giving in to the darkness.

"He fought back."

The smell of burning was almost intolerable as he awoke, head buzzing and heavy. He looked around; barely able to move his head he realised she was not at his side.

Sharply he tried to climb to his feet, stumbling and disorientated. Orange flames lit up the muddy grass. The air felt hot and giddy.

The force of the explosion had blown him far away from the building. He looked around desperately searching for Beth, no idea of how long he'd been unconscious.

He was surrounded by burning debris and he could smell burning flesh. The spawn had been blown onto the lawn yet there was no sign of Billy.

Amid the chaos he spotted her in the distance standing with her back to him, up ahead; a dark but feminine figure.

She stood watching as the thing dragged itself towards her, barely human now, its melted flesh had mostly fallen away and she could see the pure bone along the one broken arm. It was one of the spawn; jaw snapping and falling it crawled through the mud and flames towards her, pulling itself by its claws.

Its hand came to rest on her boot, and she felt disgust at the pitiful creature that somehow seemed to be still living.

Xanther stumbled over to her and he said, "Thank God you're okay."

"Look," she said, "It's still alive."

"One of their... spawn, isn't it?" he asked.

She nodded, "What if we can't beat them?"

He kicked the burning, struggling thing, causing the skull to detach and its arm to stop grabbing at Beth.

"You never did have any respect for anything..." the familiar voice growled, distorted from behind them. A sense of dread entered her heart as she slowly turned to see him rise from the rubble.

As the dark smouldering figure gradually stood to its full height, they realised it should not be alive. Its skin was black, charred and stiff, the eyes non-existent. Slowly, it raised one leg forward, then the other. A low groan emanated from somewhere within before it burst into a thousand tiny ashes, disappearing into the night air.

The couple crouched down, protecting themselves from the ash that blew through the air around them, resting on their clothes before disintegrating.

She turned to him. Realised he looked so weak she held him shakily in her arms. A single tear dropped down her cheek and onto the wreckage around them.

"We have to close the door to their world. I have to go back and face them," she said, clutching the amulet that shone a deathly pale in his eyes, "With this, I am the lock."

With a voice full of determination and regret, he replied, "We'll go together."

They advanced towards the centre of the destruction, stepping over the fallen Aime sign to reach the front foyer. Most of the spawn were dying, those still alive rendered useless by the flames and Billy's wrath. Their dying shrieks continued. Xanther had never heard anything so alien sounding in his life.

The building creaked as they entered and it felt like a new sense of being had overcome the place. She could feel the walls almost beating, and with a sense of foreboding she knew that a change was already beginning to occur. She could not let that happen, not to such a beautiful world; Orenia had become her home. Its people had welcomed her into their arms, their courage took her breath away and she felt a deep sorrow for Orenia.

Within herself, she began to prepare for her final return. After all these years, she would go home to face the Chaka.

The portal called to her. She could no longer ignore the terrible colours she knew in her heart it would hold. Xanther held her hand firmly; he had no idea what to expect of the place she was going to, so innocent he couldn't possibly bring him to understand the hell she came from.

The blast had ripped open the window to the otherworld and it stood twisted and elongated before them, large and unwelcoming. The room seemed to have taken on a life of its own, soon to be unstoppable if she left it any longer.

Beth said, "I love you, I really do – more than words could ever describe, so please, let me go and do this."

His eyes filled with tears and he held her tightly to him, "No, I can never let you go, Beth. I'm coming with you. We'll fight them together."

She started to struggle against him. First closing them off and then giving in to her emotions, she fell against him. He kissed her hair and looking up she froze in shock as she noticed his eyes had changed to a bright blue.

She had no idea when he had changed but he stood in front of her, his expression happy, but obviously perplexed. She searched those eyes, looking for a sign of something different, evil. It was as if she saw into his very soul for the first time, it was all him and nothing more, or less. It was Xanther. He was beautiful and her love for him flooded her entire being.

"It's just… your eyes," she said.

"W-what about them?" Xanther asked.

"They're blue."

He smiled, not sure what to say. The portal had started to distort and widen around them impatiently, as if growing into the very essence of space. The room was growing unsteady, the portal ready to suck them into the otherworld.

Beth recognised they had to close it fast, before it took on a life of its own. *I am the lock.*

Hesitating, she took his hand in hers. His blue eyes smiled at hers and together they walked forward, into the pool of lost souls and into eternity.

Chapter Twenty-Eight

The Aftermath

The snow had completely melted, leaving the forest looking fresh and new once more. Calmness had been restored to Fahra Point; the loss of Lucian was still quietly mourned by the settlers as they tried to return to normal.

Word had gotten back to them that Aime had been shut down and emptied, and the settlers waited to hear from their kin still in Middletown as part of the clean-up operation. The city would never return to normal but could only be re-built into something new. Perhaps that was a good thing.

Freya waited from her window, aware that some of the settlers were now afraid of her; she felt uncomfortable around them as she seemed to generate a lot of attention when she walked around the settlement alone. She had avoided leaving the wagon because of what they might think of her.

Delicately, her fingers traced along the cold glass as she watched the figures approach the settlement. She instantly recognised Sam as he limped forward with his broken leg and suddenly nothing seemed to matter as she found herself running towards him. She had forgiven him for leaving her with the settlers even though there was a point when she felt so alone.

Sam saw her running towards him and caught her in his arms, almost tumbling over because of his leg, before steadying himself.

"Hey, how are you holding up?" he asked Freya, delighted to see that she was okay.

"I missed you," she told him as they walked together towards the warm fire.

Many of the settlers had returned to Fahra Point with supplies and news of Middletown.

"I heard that this place had quite a fair share of action," he told her, his eyes kind and shining as he continued, "And you were right in the middle of it."

She nodded and as they walked together she told him of what had happened with Ulla and the settlers.

"Honey, they're just worried about you after all you went through here," he told her, "No one is afraid of you, okay?"

She reached for his hand and she took it, looking at his face and trying to figure out the look he was giving her.

"Sam," she said, "Where are my other brothers? Are they still in Middletown?"

He picked her up, put her down on top of a large rock and sat down beside her, knowing well it was time to tell her the truth.

"They're at home, honey, helping in town," he spoke softly. "Besides, I wanted to have some alone time with you so we could talk."

Freya looked at him, confused. She sensed he had something important to tell her. Her heart yearned to know.

"This place should hold a special meaning to you. It was named after your mother," he told her, letting the information sink in before continuing, "She was called Fahra and she was the most amazing person I've ever known."

Freya felt sorrow build up inside her, as she could not remember her mother... but something struck her as very strange.

"Sam, why are you talking about our mother like that?" she asked him, and before he answered she knew the true answer.

He replied, "Because I am your father, Freya."

Tears started to trickle down her face as she watched his eyes, searching them for answers. He held her close to him and he knew that at last he was prepared to be her father.

Before, he would have given his life just to be in Fahra's presence once again, to spend time with her the way things were before she was so brutally taken away.

Even now he had a clear picture of her in his mind; she had long red hair and pale skin, her tall, willowy figure and beautiful green eyes that were brighter than any eyes he'd seen before or since.

For so long he had held so little care for anything. He risked his life recklessly knowing that his little girl would be safe with the brothers that weren't really brothers at all.

Most of all, he had never stopped loving Fahra. For a long time he could not accept that his heart had not died with hers. When she left, leaving him with a baby and a broken heart, he didn't know how to cope.

As far as he knew, Freya had just about looked after herself with the help of the underground community. All the women had loved the tiny baby while Sam and the rest of the gang would go for days at a time without returning to the underground base.

When he returned he found it hard to face up to his responsibility; deep down he loved her but had never wanted to be a father, until now.

He woke up when the fighting started and the gang moved above ground, to a safe house on the outskirts of town where Freya would be safe.

Now, sitting on the rock and almost a full ten years old, she pulled away from him and he saw that she was smiling. It was then he noticed the unusual emblem that hung around her neck. It was pale and dull but there was something about it he almost recognised.

"Where did you get that?" he asked her.

"Lucian gave it to me, It's a moonstone," she told him, "It's meant to look most beautiful under the light of the moon."

Chapter Twenty-Nine

Another World

The light seemed to dance off her skin as Xanther floated in and out of consciousness. Everything seemed to take on an underwater quality as Beth smiled beside him, her long hair floating all around her beautiful face.

Beams of light lit up her face now and again, and colours faded in and out around them. He felt relaxed as he watched all this, while ever so vaguely aware, he was still holding her hand in his.

The air was thick to breathe at first, difficult, like nothing Xanther had ever experienced before. Now, he felt comfortable and amazed as they drifted together. The blue of Beth's dress seemed much more vibrant and every part of her seemed to shine, almost to glow as he watched her.

They seemed to be holding a conversation, but sleepily he realised that his mouth was not actually moving.

'It's the way here'. Her voice in his head spoke to him as if understanding his confusion. His mind seemed to darken as he remembered everything that had happened, and also his past. The smallest, most painful thoughts and feelings from long ago seemed to flood back into his mind. Things that he'd pushed out and tried to forget could not escape him now.

Beth was still smiling, but less so, as her eyes seemed to read every part of his soul and understand what no one could ever possibly understand of him before. Her eyes looked so clear under the lights, so pure and beautiful he felt he could almost drown in them. He sensed the pain she'd gone through and it almost hurt him to look deep into those eyes.

He felt her pain slowly sink into himself, as if absorbing it like a sponge. But at the same time that pain could not hurt him; he felt more content than he had ever felt in his life, so alive. Everything that had happened in his life seemed to come together and make sense.

His body felt heavy as he tried to move his arms, suspended in the colours and warmth of the atmosphere around them. She shook her head, meaning for him to relax.

Relax, just accept it, he told himself. He was beginning to understand that nothing was solid or certain and everything around him was not part of his world. He felt slightly delirious as he shut his eyes once more, the image of Beth beside him, filling his heart with love.

The pressure seemed to build around them and Xanther could feel the space closing in on them, the light somehow getting brighter. He could see something dark in the distance, standing out now between all the colours.

Sounds seemed to fade and mix around them, no one sound detectable from the rest. He couldn't make anything out as he imagined he heard voices in the space around them, behind them, in front of them.

The feeling of air seemed to rush past his ears and he noticed Beth looking away and then back into his eyes once more.

He had no idea how long they were in that state, or even what was real or his imagination; only the image of her beauty stayed in his mind, a promise that at least the memory was real.

Is this real? Are we really here? He heard himself ask these things, though his lips did not move. As he opened his eyes, Beth's smile grew wider and he heard her voice, fainter now in his mind reply, '*It's real. But no, not yet.*'

The darker colour loomed ahead of them as Xanther started to see the brightness that lay within it. He wanted to reach out to it, feel it the way he remembered from somewhere he could not quite remember. *Was it a dream?* he thought to himself.

It felt somehow heavy upon them, although they had not reached it, yet it drew upon his heart and he could feel it there within him.

He realised her words were once again in his head and he realised she sounded scared yet brave. She spoke to him of her world, of the Chaka and what she felt for him, her love for him and her courage. She was talking fast, yet when he looked into her eyes he knew the words were coming from her very soul. Her lips still did not move.

The vibrant darkness was so close now, almost filling the atmosphere around them like smoke. He saw it rush around Beth, in between the strands of her long dark hair and instantly over her smooth pale skin and then gone again. Her eyes never once left his as he started to breathe in the smoke around them, taking on an entirely new quality.

He started to fall into unconsciousness as the darkness enveloped them in its grasp. As his eyes got heavier and started to fall, he heard Beth's screams fade further and further away from him as if she was being carried away by the smoke or by waves in a dark sea. He let go of his confusion and entered the black.

A long low cry was the first thing he heard as he started to gather his thoughts, seemingly still emerged in the black smoke. When he started to remember the journey and the darkness, his hand immediately reached out for Beth and found nothing.

Quickly he opened his eyes as he realised he'd let her go, lost in the soothing smoke that took her away from him.

But she lay beside him in a deep sleep. Her hair fallen around her looked as smooth as silk, her torn dress once again dark and worn out. The paleness of her skin contrasted with the deep red rock that she lay on and he realised then that they were now in her world.

In the sky, he saw an old friend; a deep purple moon stared down at him and with slow dread he realised that this was the land from his dream. The skies were a dark grey mixed with purple and red. Around him for miles he saw black sand and red rocks like the one he and Beth lay on. Black dry things stuck out of the sand as if they had once been trees, just like in his dream.

A large red mountain stood far in the distance ahead of them. Slashed with orange and brown colours it stood out as something magnificent. The air was hot and humid, yet unlike in his dream he found the air easy on his lungs in this alien land.

He remembered the things Beth had told him, had shared with him during the strange journey and wondered if they had been nothing but a dream. But he knew they were real, her mind closed to him now.

He reached out to hold her delicate fingers as she lay peacefully beside him. Her hand started to move slowly as he watched her awaken from her sleep. Her eyes opened cautiously before she realised where she was. Startled, she jumped back from him, looking around at the place that had once been her home.

"Oh my God," she whispered, "For so long I have had nightmares about this place, comforting but terrifying nightmares."

Her voice soothed him, as if it had taken on a new quality in the air around them. She looked more beautiful than she ever had before, as if her life shone so much brighter and, for the first time, he really took in the knowledge that she was not in fact human but something else. Her eyes met his and she looked so incredibly unnatural in the light of the purple moon, like nothing he could remember before about her. She was different in this land, so perhaps he was too.

"Beth," the words caught in his throat and he stumbled on what to say to her. What he wanted was to protect her more than anything although deep inside he knew that she was the strong one, and all he could do was accompany her on this strange but necessary mission.

Another low cry uttered from the sky, making him shiver in the hot air.

"Don't worry," she told him, her voice like cool milk in the heat around him. "They can't hurt you, those are the tacholyns."

From the name, he knew it was the thing he saw in his dream, the bony, dead skeletal thing that flapped across the landscape. Whether or not it was his imagination, he could hear it flapping those wings now.

"Ignore them," Beth continued as she laced up one of her boots, now worn and falling to bits around her slim, bruised leg, "We've got bigger problems to deal with."

He looked at her and she returned his gaze, before uttering the words, "The Chaka know we're here. They're waiting for us."

Instinctively he looked towards the mountain that seemed to be calling him and at once he knew they must travel in its direction; he dreaded what was about to come.

"I dreamt about this place too," he told her. "What is that mountain?"

"It's somewhere almost… sacred to us. You can feel it, can't you? It pulls us; we must go through it to face them. They lie in wait, but trust me."

"Always," he replied, his attention once again drawn to the mountain that seemed to know him, like an old friend.

"Be careful, Xanther," Beth grabbed hold of his arm, snapping him back to reality, her eyes glowing intensely, "It is hungry for life."

Together they walked through the black sands, through nests of dead trees and over red plains and hard rocks. In the distance, the cries of the tacholyns echoed through the dead world. Sometimes other sounds would follow, like the high-pitched moans that sounded almost insane. At first they unsettled him, seeming so close that they could jump out from behind a rock to harm them but Beth's steely resistance drove him to ignore the sounds of the alien world.

He had many questions; he wanted to know what had happened there, so long ago to make it into the world it now was. If the Chaka had not been so hungry for destruction, what would this place look like now?

Strangely he could still sense life around him, the dead world filled with sounds and what should be ghosts. It made him greatly uneasy. Beth squeezed his hand as if sensing his discomfort, the air around them heating as they walked further inland towards the red-blotted landscape and the beauty of the purple moon.

Chapter Thirty

Dead Awakening

They had walked over dry shores of black sands, rocks and gorges until they'd found a worn-out line in the sand. It was barely visible, nevertheless wide enough to tell that it had once been a path, long after the seas had dried up.

Beth's attention focused ahead of her, towards the calling place she had fled many years ago. A hint of silver caught the light in the corner of Xanther's eye, and as he looked down he noticed she had wrapped the silver chain around her wrist and around her hand, the amulet glowing brightly as it hung from the chain twisted around her fingers. It looked different now, as if filled with a liquid amber that boiled deep down inside.

Not understanding why she had taken it from around her neck, he reached out to take her hand. She cringed away, and it was then he saw the red burn on her palm.

"The stone burns you, doesn't it?" he asked her.

"Yes, in this world it pains to touch it," she said, looking at him solemnly.

He reached out as it to take it from her, but she held her hand away from him.

"No," she told him, "This is my burden alone to bear."

There was barely a breeze in the warm air around them as they approached a group of dead trees. Black and burnt-out it was clear they had died long ago. It was only when they got closer that Xanther saw the black pool, thick like tar on the ground.

Something else lay close by it; dark and stained. He made out an arm that had once been clothed in white, burnt.

"What the hell is that?" Xanther whispered, trying to work out what could possibly have happened, his mind going blank.

The arm slowly started to move, the darkly-stained body becoming visible as it shakily pulled itself along the sand towards the couple.

What Xanther saw would burn in his mind forever, the horror of the thing that was supposed to be dead but somehow wasn't.

Its skin was a rotting brown and somehow Xanther knew what it was; the once-white coat now darkened and mostly burnt away by the pool of tar and the harshness of their world.

Unexplainably it crawled forward. An inhuman moan that hurt his ears emanated from deep within its failed vocal chords, jaw slowly opening yet it had no lips to form the words. Xanther didn't believe it could have spoken anyway. It was close to them now, although its eyes were long gone, melted in the heat from the tar.

They watched as it started to rise up on its legs, the flesh eaten away. Bare bone was exposed through the burnt and torn fabric of the trouser. Shakily it tried to move forward but fell back onto the black sand once more.

A name badge hung off the ruined lab coat and barely able to make out the letters Xanther read the name; 'P.D Manson'.

How it could hold life inside its vile carcass, he didn't even want to think but the reality was its grasping hand reaching out for him and for Beth. Some of the flesh had been melted away leaving bits of bone, dirty and exposed.

"Kill it," Beth whispered under her breath.

Xanther looked confused as he mouthed back, '*how*'. He stepped back as its hand touched his frayed black jeans.

Beth swiftly took a step forward and kicked the rotting head, kicking it hard. It instantly detached from the rest of its body, almost entirely unrecognisable as human. The body seemed to slow then come to a stop, the jaw snapping shut a few feet away from the rest of its body.

Beth looked down at the mess that lay in front of them and slowly shook her head, as if deeply disappointed by the thing's unwillingness to die.

"It's one of the lab researchers," she spoke softly, "He must have chosen to enter the portal."

"Hey, you're learning fast… is it dead?" Xanther asked her.

"God, I hope so, but nothing here really dies…" she replied. Looking at Xanther's pale face it looked almost purple in the light of the moon.

The laughter rose up all around them, seemed to echo through their ears and, confused, Xanther could at first see nothing but the same plain landscape that they'd travelled through for what felt like hours.

It was a cruel, almost insane laugh that seemed to originate from more than one being. The source was almost undetectable until he felt a cold wind pass through his hair, like icy fingertips caressing him in a terrible way.

When he first saw them, he thought they were barely real, like silvery smoke in the air. But they were moving and laughing, their faces changing in the light.

One of them reached out to him as if calling him, and he stepped back from its gaze. They moved far too quickly, barely there but malevolent in their presence.

Amongst the laughter he heard Beth's voice as they gathered around her, creating a cold wind that he couldn't have imagined in the humid atmosphere of the dried-out landscape.

She was chanting something very quickly, her hair blowing around her harshly as the spirits encompassed her. He tried to reach her, but was blown back by the cruel force of the spirit wind.

Suddenly the silvery figures darted back, and he heard Beth shout, "Leave us be!"

"Beth!" Xanther shouted to her, as one of the spirits turned its attention on him. Before she could do a thing to stop it, it rushed towards him with such force it knocked him back on the ground, its coldness going straight through his body and chilling him to the bone.

He screamed as cold, pure pain seized through his body like nothing he had ever felt before. Then it was gone, leaving only coldness and confusion.

Beth ran towards him, and he vaguely heard her scream his name, demanding to know if he was all right. He nodded as he slowly began to gather his thoughts, Beth holding him closely, her eyes bright with fear and what could have only been anger.

Later he would find the scar where he had cut his arm from the fall, the alien substance already beginning to course through his veins.

Closer than ever, the mountain loomed ahead of them, shining a dull red through Xanther's human eyes. The air had already begun to cool around them as the sky started to darken to a deep blue, blotted with grey and black.

Beth grasped his hand and immediately she knew what he was thinking – that whatever they had to face was there, waiting for them.

A sense of panic was already slowly starting to build up inside her; so long ago had she escaped from the Chaka. She had managed to ward off the spirits, but the rest would not prove to be a light battle.

She looked at Xanther, his unusual blue eyes shining into hers and she knew one thing; she was terrified for his soul.

Together they headed towards the mountainside, a rough-but-safe enough place for them to rest while their hosts prepared for a great balance.

Chapter Thirty-One

Freya's Dream

Although it had been days since she'd left the settlement with Sam – she couldn't bear to call him 'dad', at least not yet – she found herself back in the forest that night. It was dark and silent apart from the wildlife that hid from her sight behind plants and trees and darkness.

She felt a soft breeze caress her and as she walked forward she heard the faintest voice call her name, '*Freya*'. It was female and as soon as she heard it a thought entered the furthest reaches of her mind.

She could smell the lake ahead of her and something told her to move forward, towards the opening in the trees not too far ahead.

She welcomed the cool air on her hot skin, savouring it as her hands moved through the thick leaves around her, pulling some of them away from the trees. In her left hand she grasped the emblem, the stone she'd kept a secret from the settlers that night when Lucian was taken. For some reason it seemed important that she'd kept it, although it had never once glowed as it had done that night. Then, in the dream that didn't feel like a dream, she knew that its dulling sleep would be temporary.

The forest was still deep-rooted in her mind; the texture of the leaves felt smooth at the touch of her fingertips and as she scrunched them up in her palm, she savoured the feeling. The breeze soothed her, the darkness of the night strangely welcoming, like an old friend. But something in the forest was not welcoming, the presence of someone she knew but at the same time couldn't possibly know... could she?

She hesitated as she reached the end of the trees, peering out onto the lake. At first she could not fathom the sight that lay before her, out on the edge of the lake under the light of the moon.

It was a woman with pale white skin and long red hair; she sat on the only rock that looked out to the lake, her back facing the forest and Freya. She was completely naked, although her hair covered some of her nakedness.

Freya knew almost instantly the thought that she'd been harbouring deep down inside her mind, the one that the breeze had stirred deep inside her. Now it was something she could not ignore, as Fahra, her mother was there before her very eyes, waiting silently.

Part of Freya wanted to go to her right then and she started to step forward, her hands shaking by her sides.

She knew something was not right about this scene; she'd never remembered her mother, never knew her. Still the woman sat facing the lake, her body did not stir.

Freya wanted to speak to her, ask her where she'd been but her voice locked up as she found herself moving forward towards the rock. So many questions filled her mind, unable to trust the moment fear started to well up from a deep place inside her soul.

Her footsteps were audible on the pebbles and she was now sure the woman could hear her, knew she was there. Then all of a sudden the woman's posture changed, seemed to tense as if hearing her for the first time.

For a second Freya felt the stone in the left hand grow so hot that it burned her hand, so much so that she let the leaves she'd gathered drop to the ground. The burning was gone, the stone already losing its glow that had momentarily burned bright in her grasp.

The woman that was her mother only sat a few feet away now, as she slowly turned her head round to face her daughter.

Freya felt numb all over, unable to take her eyes away from the sight. Her mother's face was undoubtedly beautiful, with vibrant green eyes and full rosy lips which quickly turned into a nasty snarl of aggression which chilled Freya's heart.

Her eyes seemed to burn into Freya's as she moved round on the rock, naked her stance recoiled like an angry wolf or perhaps more like a snake. Her nails were long and seemed to scrape on the rock, her eyes now drawn to Freya's left hand.

Freya had made up her mind to run when the woman's voice broke her thoughts completely.

"My darling girl," the woman-beast spoke in a voice that was most definitely human but undoubtedly cold and cruel. "What are you going to do with that? You are a fool if you think you can win any wars with that *thing*."

"It's…it's mine," Freya told her, unable to move from the spot she was standing in despite the woman's, her mother's burning eyes. She was unable to look away from those eyes.

"Give it to me," Fahra hissed as she moved forward from her perch on the rock. Freya shook her head, grasping the stone even tighter in her hand.

Her mother repeated the words, *"Give it to me… or throw it in the river yourself!"* Her teeth were sharpened into white little points and as she stepped off the rock there was something animalistic about her. She started to move towards Freya, not quite steady on her two feet. There was something very powerful about her, yet she managed to also look clumsy and slightly pathetic as if she did not belong in this world anymore.

"No!" Freya shouted. For some reason the instinct came to her to hold up the precious stone in the direction of Fahra, causing the creature to recoil in what looked like pain.

"Don't you dare use that on me," the mother-thing snarled at Freya, with inhuman eyes. But Freya was determined to stop it from approaching her, as never in this world could this thing be her mother.

It was then she noticed the tiny black movements on the ground, coming up from behind Fahra. They weren't quite ants or spiders as they looked like tiny black stars, making the earth around them come alive with movement. They started to creep up Fahra's pale, thin legs. What happened next happened fast.

They had come from the lake and quickly they encircled her, seemingly pulling her back towards the water, quickly covering her smooth skin until only her face was left. She screamed a most terrible, haunting scream that sounded violent and filled with anger before chanting something that Freya found familiar but alien. She staggered back against their force, towards the dark water of the lake.

Freya saw the water was black with them as she was immersed in the lake, her chanting moans muffled and then gone, evaporated in the water.

Freya stepped towards the edge of the lake as the water seemed to calm; all traces of the things had disappeared from the pebbles. The water looked clear as she leaned down and touched it with her hand.

She froze as she caught sight of her reflection; long red hair, pale skin and angry green eyes. She blinked, and all she could see was herself again, a small girl with young, scared eyes and blonde curly hair.

The water felt slimy on her fingers and at some point she realised that she was not at the lake anymore; she was lying in bed, looking up at the ceiling.

Her heart beat fast in her chest and as she looked around the room, her eye caught on the glow in the corner. It was the emblem, the only bright thing in the room.

The glow quickly vanished and she was left in the dark once more and for just a second she heard Fahra's lingering moans ever so softly fading into the distance. The first thing that entered her mind was Sam.

Vincent sat staring into the fire, unable to reach a state of sleep. It was 3am, the house full of friends who were unavoidably homeless. Many of the underground dwellers needed a place to stay while reconstruction work was carried out. Some had moved temporarily out of town, while most were taken in by the kindness of the town folk.

Strangely, the terrible incident which had brought so much death and pain had also served a good purpose; it had brought the community closer together in a way they had not seen in years.

At the house, many of their friends slept in sleeping bags and bedding laid out on the living room floor and the bedrooms were full. Most of the occupants would be helping to clear the underground the next day, just like the day before and the day before that.

Vincent hoped the underground community would be wider and better than ever before, open to everybody unlike the divide it had once caused. Others opposed the rebuilding and protests were made about the memorial it would serve to all that had died there.

Most of all it was about returning to normal.

Sam joined Vincent at the fire; his eyes looked tired and sad. He was still wearing the clothes he'd worn all day, only just returning from the destruction site.

"Are you okay?" he asked Vincent.

"Yeah… can't sleep," Vincent replied, glancing at Sam briefly before his eyes returned to the fire.

"I know. I worked all day and all night. Now I'm back here, I can't even think of sleep because everything out there's still moving, they're still working…and Beth."

Vincent knew how Sam felt, but that wasn't why he could not sleep; he was scared of his dreams. Some nights he saw the explosion all over again, only this time Sam and Daire had died, or Beth, or even Freya who wasn't even there when it happened. Although he knew this wasn't real, it terrified him what could have happened that day. He had already lost Marcus, one of his closest friends, and was afraid of what was to come. When he first found out about Marcus, it was like he had already known deep down what had happened. So many people around him were facing the loss of loved ones and friends that his mourning seemed so unimportant and so much harder to deal with. But pushing it down inside just made him sleepless and haunted. He couldn't help think that he'd let Marcus down.

Beth and Xanther had been gone for a while and until they returned he couldn't know if things were over or predict what was still to come.

"Sam," Vincent said, "Don't work there tomorrow. Make sure Freya's okay; she needs you."

Sam nodded, quietly contemplating his brother's mood before silently stepping over the sleeping bags – and people – to make his way finally to bed.

Lydia was asleep next to Vincent; her soft rhythmic breathing calmed him as he smiled at her lying there so innocently. He knew then he wanted to protect her against whatever was to happen.

Her fingers moved as if dreams had overtaken her sleep, he reached out to touch them. Her face stayed calm and soothing to his mind and he realised at last he wanted to sleep. For the first time in days he felt like he belonged right there, beside her in the crowded, warm house.

As he lay down next to her, a smile appeared across his friend's face and she moved close to him before drifting off to sleep once more.

The warmth of her embrace made him feel at ease as they lay there beside the dying flames of the fireplace. Thoughts still raced through his mind, but they soon left him one by one as he eventually fell into a deep, silent sleep.

Chapter Thirty-Two

The Reckoning

The darkness had fallen upon them like a thick black tide sweeping in over the sands, bringing with it unimaginable creatures that would look alien if the light of day were ever to touch them.

Their shrieks filled the skies, the crunch of bones and flapping of heavy wings accompanying the howling noises of the winds. If he listened hard enough, he could sometimes make out words in the howling, even once hearing his own name.

Xanther could barely see Beth as she sat across from him, sheltered under a crevice in the mountain cave. He was aware, from Beth's words and actions that they were close to the holy place of the Chaka.

She had told him that when the world dawned, they would reach the pool of Dalakra where she must face them alone. If all failed, they would not be able to return to Orenia, instead would be stuck in Beth's world.

Her words stuck in his mind: *I must reach the pool of Dalakra, where you must stand down. I will face them alone, and when the amulet meets the holy water it will be destroyed and all will become unstable. The portal may open for us then, but I will stay here forever if escaping means letting them through to Orenia. I am the lock…*

The amulet glowed deeply in the darkness of the cave. It lay on the ground but Xanther imagined the silver of the chain still rested around Beth's wrist.

Beth was deadly serious, her eyes barely shining in the glow from the amulet. She spoke quietly from time to time, and Xanther wondered inexplicably if she'd changed somehow during the night, if her world had somehow clutched her once again, recognised her as its own. If it was something minor that was affecting her – which he hoped it was – then it would be gone by morning. A nagging feeling told him that maybe it was 'Them'. He wanted to reach out and touch her, but he realised that he was afraid of her reaction.

His mind seemed fragile, memories of the past few hours blurred somewhat. It was as if he'd cut out some of the sights he'd seen, unable to take in the alien background. Perhaps it was having an effect on him more than it ever could on Beth.

"Xanther," he heard Beth whisper to him under her breath, "Stay close. Don't listen to their sounds."

"Okay," he replied, slightly confused. He felt slightly dazed, as if his body was reacting to the very air he was breathing – he realised this was most likely. He saw Beth's lips curl into a smile in the darkness of the cave.

She held up her arm, the stone revealing more of her face, "Do you see it? It's glowing brightly now."

As she smiled, he momentarily caught sight of one small, sharp white tooth; her eyes gleamed hauntingly and flashed golden for just a second. *Trick of the light,* Xanther thought, although what he saw stuck in his mind.

Beth seemed not to notice, her thoughts overtaking themselves he could tell she was deeply moved by the world she'd for so long tried to forget.

"Why is it glowing like that? Why does its touch burn you?" he asked her.

"This world has made it come alive once more," she replied. "Although it responds to the Chaka, it also hurts me to touch its glow because even though I escaped their world, I am still part of them."

"This," she said, holding the amulet, "Could make their world collapse, and I'll hold it against anyone who tries to stop me. It must be destroyed."

Her voice sounded so full of regret as she admitted her roots, although it was nothing he hadn't known before. Nothing could ever make him fear her because she was beautiful, strong and good, unlike the evil that had haunted her for so long after she had escaped her home.

What she kept from Xanther that night, was how incredibly terrified she was of confronting the Chaka once more. They would try to keep her in their world, would take her away from those she loved. Orenia, her home for so many years, had decreased her power, her memories of the Chaka blocked from her mind as if it had been a distant nightmare – only they had served her reminders through the loss of her friends and the love that at the time had seemed like the most important part of her – something that had been cruelly taken away from her. She knew better now. Beth was so much weaker in their world but her hatred for them grew deep down inside her like a dark twisted monster that yearned to be set free. Soon it would be.

The strong winds seemed to rage even louder, as Xanther moved closer to her. She was thankful he was there beside her, but scared she would lose him and sorry that she'd endangered his beautiful soul, so innocent to her ever-changing eyes.

His eyes searched hers; unable to tell what burdens she kept hidden under her smile. They kissed softly, as he held her close to him and she let go of her thoughts in his arms.

The next time he opened his eyes, Xanther found himself beside Beth who seemed to be sleeping. Her eyes were shut and her face was calm, carried away with the force of her dreams.

The winds seemed to have settled and the cave was eerily silent, the darkness still shrouding the view of the landscape outside. Beth's chain had fallen off her wrist and the glow of the amulet seemed to be dying. As it went out, he heard a harsh whisper calling his name, *"Xanther"*.

He had a sudden urge to stand, as if the voice was leading him out of the cave and away from Beth. He looked at her, peacefully sleeping and barely visible in the darkness, her hair falling heavily over her face, her arm stretched out beside the amulet. He resisted the strange need to take it from her, as slowly he stood up.

Outside, he could no longer see the purple of the moon, the sky almost devoid of all colour.

As he stepped onto the black sand once more, he realised he felt a chill in the air. It made him shiver.

He heard it in his ear, *'you'll never take her'* the harsh voice hissed. He felt the coldness plunge through him as he staggered aside, trying to find a way out of the cold spot.

Voices all around him started to chant, a strange alien language that caught in his heart. The voices all seemed to meld into one, confusing him and giving him the feeling of being surrounded.

His head felt heavy as his eyes searched around in the darkness, unable to see the source of the whispers. One voice seemed to emerge as being louder than all the rest. It told him:

'The Dalakra charm is ours; we shall never let you destroy it, human. Leave this world before your soul becomes ours. Beth is one of our own and she will take your soul as well as sacrificing her own. Leave our child...'

"She's not your child anymore!" he screamed angrily as cold pain ripped through his body. He was determined to protect Beth even if it meant sacrificing himself.

In response to his courage, their laughter shrieked all around him, and he could just about make out the silvery lines as he felt them all around him, like harsh angry winds.

"Take me. Do what you like but leave her be! Send her back to Orenia where she belongs!"

The laughter stopped abruptly as the more prominent voice became cruel and angry.

'You think that is where she belongs, do you? Let us show you what she really is!"

He gasped for breath as the powerful forces seemed to draw closer around him, their coldness making his whole body go numb. They seemed to encircle him almost like a hurricane and he felt himself drawn up by their energy.

He could see them now, not just the silver of the smoke-like figures but colours. They seemed to become more vivid as they spun around him, and he saw at once that they were not at all human.

Their forms were tall, faces so pale their skin took on a sort of cobweb-like quality as if he couldn't always see where the lines of their face began. Their teeth were sharp points in their cruel smiles, eyes burning deep violet, shining the way he'd never have imagined a human's eyes to look.

He saw the world in the light. It was full of vibrant colours that looked more beautiful than he could describe. It was in the past, and he saw Beth with the others. She looked different, more like them but still beautiful, with a beauty that only she could possess.

Her eyes shone the same gold as the Chaka as they joined together upon one of their own people. Frightened, the female struggled and shouted in their words as the gang pounced upon her. Harshly, one of them ripped open her belly and the alien blood spilled out onto the earth. Beth joined in as they savagely filled their blood-thirst and dreadful hunger for the soul.

Xanther could not look away as he was forced to watch the terrible struggle for replenishment. The voice spoke to him, harshly but with seeming enjoyment.

'She destroyed her own kind,' it spoke clearly in his ear, *'she may claim not to be one of us, but when her hunger took over she killed with brutal strength, greed and power. When our world began to dry up and we'd taken all the souls of the next, we were forced to feed upon our own. So now you learn the truth.'*

"No!" Xanther screamed, "It's not true!"

The laughter echoed all around him until it hurt his ears, the scene fading away around him as he landed on the dark sand, body exhausted.

He looked up to see Beth, standing ahead of him and looking shocked in the glow of the amulet. The winds seemed to settle around them, the laugher drifting off towards the mountain.

She ran to him, throwing herself onto his chilled and tired body. She looked furious, towards the mountain as she sensed their presence.

"How dare you show him what you forced me to do! I hate you, *cowards*!" She started to scream words he could never understand before breaking down in tears. Sobbing, she ran her warm hand through Xanther's hair.

"God, you're so cold," she whispered, "Come on, let's get back to shelter. I should never have slept."

She helped him to stand and together they walked the short distance to the cave. Looking at her now, he saw the same Beth that he loved, despite the flash of gold that he noticed every so often in her eyes. She noticed him looking, her expression worried and wounded at what he had seen.

When they reached their hiding place she held him closely to her, sharing the heat of her body as she searched his eyes for some sort of reaction.

"What you saw... that's why I left this world, their cruelty... surrounded by death and intolerable hunger it was too much for me to bear," she told him.

"Beth," he replied, trying to find the words, "You don't have to explain yourself to anyone."

Her face was wet with tears as she remembered with sorrow what their world had once been like. The shame of her actions, the taking of life from every outlet was now visible on her still human face.

He traced a finger over her tears, gently wiping them away as he held her in his arms. Together they reached deep that night for even the slightest of comfort and finding it in each other, clutched it tight never to let go.

When Xanther sleepily opened his eyes, unaware of his working mind through dreams that had been kept hidden, light was creeping into the shallow cave and dawn welcomed him. It was calm now, no uninviting wind or sounds of the night creatures lingered.

Beth was still close to his side and he savoured the last few moments of being near to her before she left the world of slumber. She looked rested; her strength gathered inside her strong yet delicate frame, her long hair looking dusty from the sand on the ground.

In time, the pair left the cave together, looking up at the vast mountains that stood tall before them. The moon shone above them, a vibrant purple that made everything look slightly different to his eyes. He continued to marvel at the beautiful yet foreboding world, Beth's world.

She looked tired and most definitely unnatural under the purple light, the amulet once again hanging from her small wrist.

It glowed with life, illuminating her skin making it look as pure as milk.

A small change had occurred within her during the night; after what happened, she was no longer deeply terrified of the Chaka. She had confronted her past through Xanther, and now it felt almost as if a great weight had been lifted from her shoulders, revealing a newfound courage from her tomb of regret for this world.

To Xanther, it showed as she looked into his eyes and he knew that she was ready.

Their journey towards the centre of the mountain would begin by travelling upwards, towards the entrance of the cave that would lead them to the sacred pool.

Many of Beth's dreams had centred on that very place, the heart of the Chaka that lay in the mountain and the land that continued from it.

It was a place that she'd never imagined to see again, where children like her were born and also put to rest. The amulet which hung from her wrist, which burned her skin and held a great power deep inside the unrelenting stone had once been made from the pool of Dalakra. It was a survivor of the keys shaped to hold doors for their world, never again to be returned to the sacred pool that bore life as well as welcomed death.

Beth realised that now was the time to seal their world as the amulet grew ever more volatile in its atmosphere. When it became one with the pool, she could only guess the consequences of her faith and perhaps…yes, perhaps hope.

Her memory of the mountain was vague yet something – maybe memories buried deep in her soul or perhaps guidance from the elder spirits – led her towards the hidden paths that lay embedded to guide the travellers.

At the start of the climb, the mountain appeared dead and dry. The rocks were bare and black sand partially covered the ancient walkways. Around mid-way, it took on a new shape with dark green grass and signs of plants that grew close to the ground. Small crevasses began to appear surrounded by the vegetation and dark, soft shapes grew that appeared to Xanther as flowers.

As they began to walk downwards her eyes widened as all her memories came flooding back to her, the spiral towards the centre, welcoming her once more.

It had been a place she had hated yet was bound to; somewhere she'd been forced to love. The dark sharp rocks, the screams, the worship and so-called learning of the ancient world. And them. They controlled everything, fighting for the last of the keys to quell their hunger for blood, for souls and torture, cruelty and despair.

Her fingers gripped the side of the rock firmly as she tried to force the memories away with the pain, fighting the visions that haunted her mind.

"Beth," Xanther exclaimed desperately, trying to lift her bleeding hand away from the rock.

"Beth, stop please!"

With surprise she stared at him wide-eyed, before looking at the blood on her shaking hand. Although Xanther could not tell, she knew it was becoming their blood once more, inhuman, alien.

Forcing herself to remain calm, she nodded and whispered, "Come on, we don't have much time."

Together, they entered the enclosed space of the spiral, surrounded by the dark rock and soft, but somehow wrong texture of the flowers that grew from it. Xanther felt one of them on his neck, making his skin crawl. Quickly he brushed it off and feeling his neck, noticed the unpleasant residue it had left on his skin.

It seemed to go on forever, the darkness encompassing them and leaving them blind to what lay before them deeper into the mountain. The amulet's light seemed blocked by the blackness in the cave.

At some point Beth realised she could hear the trickle of water, knowing without knowing that it was the sacred water of Dalakra. It had not touched her skin for so many years, and now it called her deep within the mountain; it knew her.

She felt a great presence in the darkness; the spirits of all those she had loved and lost in such a cruel world. It scared her to think of what they could possibly think of her.

They reached the bottom and were met by the silvery water of the pool. It illuminated the underground cave in a way that Xanther had never expected.

Beth's heart now went out to it, and all the years of love came back into her mind. A single tear began to creep down her cheek, the amulet burning brighter than ever before.

"Is this it?" Xanther asked, to which she nodded in response.

"It's so beautiful, isn't it?" she replied in a voice full of sadness and regret.

The cave was large, leading upwards towards the light at the opposite side of the mountain. Xanther could feel something inside him stir as he looked around at the unsettling movements in the walls. Small pictures and symbols were carved into the stone, and in the corner of his eyes they seemed almost to come alive, to beckon him.

Their voices filled the cave, those of the dead. They spoke deeply, almost as in an ancient song that echoed through Xanther's mind. Beth immersed herself in their language, her eyes closed. She raised the amulet to the level of her face.

It seemed to respond to voices, a bright light emanating from the stone and lighting up the whole cave, filling it with a golden colour. The cave seemed to be accumulating energy. The voices grew louder and faster, and a smile appeared on Beth's face.

They were interrupted by a loud scream. It filled the cave, and took away the light leaving only the shallow glow of the amulet and the silver water that seemed to breathe with life.

Xanther was forced back against the cave wall, unable to move closer to Beth as she stood still in the darkness. By the glow of the amulet he could make out the outline of her long hair and pale shoulder.

The screams hurt his ears. They were louder than ever before and as he tried to cover his ears all he could think of was Beth. The ancient room seemed to fill with the coldness of the Chaka, the spirits circling around her in the dark. They seemed so much stronger in the sanctity of the cave, so much so that it took Xanther's breath away. It felt like a giant, terrible weight was pushing on his chest and suddenly he found it difficult to breathe. He turned cold, his fingers struggling against the wall behind him yet he could not break free from the hold. The wall was rough and damp; it seemed to vibrate as if the whole cave was coming alive. He imagined it was awakening from a deep sleep.

Their noise clouded Beth head as she stood strong, daring one of them to come close enough to the amulet. It felt like the only warmth in the room, so close to her own skin yet not touching, it felt like a strange comfort.

Under her breath she whispered in their language, words she had not used in what seemed like forever.

Barely audible within the sounds of chanting and howls she heard their footsteps, quick and agile, enter the cave.

'Sariama, you seek to destroy us,' a cold, cruel voice spoke up as if using the voice of a thousand souls. It spoke just a few feet away from where she was standing, the darkness cloaking what was her worst enemy.

'So you have nothing to say, traitor' the voice hissed and snarled, angrily spitting words out that Beth instantly recognised yet sent a chill down her spine.

"Come closer, *Gharisha*. Show your face to me one last time…" Beth spoke softly, coldly whilst ever so slightly lifting the amulet in front of her, "Or are you afraid?"

'I could never be afraid of you, little girl,' it spoke as a dark shape materialised out of the darkness, getting closer to Beth's position.

She could hear its breath, rasping and old yet she knew she could also smell blood; the Chaka were still feeding.

As the thing came closer, Beth's nightmares suddenly came true as she looked upon the face that had haunted her, followed her to Orenia and burnt deep down in her mind. The faces of her loved ones came back to her, those she had lost due to the hands of the evil creature that lay before her. Emma, Silvia, Tristan… she was a murderer perhaps, cold-blooded. Well that was a point of view. But one thing she could not be, oh no, not to them, was forgiving. Anger raged up inside her, the pain washing away as she felt a power surge run through her body.

Now the face of her tormentor looked ugly, aged and dry with eyes that had whitened and clouded severely, making the once powerful creature take on the look of the blind.

Its blood red lips were curled into a snarl to reveal sharp points of teeth, its claws outstretched as it tried to snatch the amulet from Beth's wrist.

It screamed in pain as the amulet burned the creature's wrinkled skin. The chain snapped and it fell to the floor taking the light with it.

"Beth!" Xanther screamed, unable to see her in the darkness of the cave.

'Quiet, mortal boy,' the main voice snapped, *'This is not your battle to fight. You follow her to our holy land and to your death!'*

The water started to bubble, movement visible underneath the illuminating glow and he knew that he was witnessing; birth.

Beth snatched the amulet, allowing it to burn her skin. She winced in pain as she held it above the water.

"You'll never escape this world again, because I have the key and I'm going to use it, destroy it and destroy you!" She screamed. The Chaka beast snarled hungrily, its awkward body once tall but now crooked drew itself up taller than little Beth.

'No, child, you'll stay here, locked with us forever until you starve like the rest of us, enduring this hell for eternity! Our world is dead now and no longer do we need blood...if we have you.'

It lunged forward, shrieking with malevolence. The others were behind. One of them threw fire towards Beth which lit up the cave and separated the cold air of the spirits. Xanther saw her fall back as she dropped the amulet into the pool. Immediately it turned black and his head filled with pain.

He realised it was that of the Chaka, their screams loud and desperate as a hand, already turning black reached out of the pool, melting onto the rock.

Deep within the water grew something light, a bright white circle in the very centre of the pool. He frowned, feeling it call to him.

He found the strength to separate himself from the cave wall, running towards Beth and the creature which was now coiled up in pain.

It seemed to be turning into the smoke that had tormented him and tried to remove him from Beth. Its eyes melted down its face and onto the hard rock of the cave.

He could see the others now, running towards the entrance, to the light where he knew the moon would be waiting.

Beth shouted, "Quick, we have to jump into the pool. The portal's starting to close!"

It all became clear; the white light was in fact the portal that led back to his home, Orenia.

Quickly he helped Beth to her feet, grasping her hand firmly in his. He could feel the portal, knew exactly what it would be like to immerse himself in it once more. He imagined Orenia, full of beauty and friends. He looked at Beth, weak now she looked as if she would collapse in his arms.

"Are you ready?" he asked her.

Before she could answer, the blind thing lunged at her once more, trying to pull her to the ground. Its awful moans became muffled as its teeth tried to sink into her skin.

Xanther pulled it away and with some unknown strength managed to throw it onto the hard ground, before holding Beth in his arms.

"We need to go… the portal," she whispered, barely able to speak, her breath shallow in her chest.

He took a deep breath as he held onto her tight and prepared to take a leap into the whiteness that would soon disappear forever from the harsh alien world.

He jumped.

It was like returning home, a place he never wanted to leave. Its comfort filled every part of him, making him feel so incredibly free. His breaths came easy and light, the healing power of the vortex soothing his mind and allowing him to forget the cold and anything wrong or cruel in the world. He felt his body fill up with light, once again surrendering to its power.

Has it worked? he thought. Unable to think properly, his confused state allowed him only to linger on Beth.

He watched her long hair shining and clean in the water-like substance. Her eyes were filled with pain, and flashed gold into his. Her dress, unfortunately, had not survived the monstrosity well; it was torn in several places which gave it an even more surreal quality.

Her hand had been permanently marked by the oval shape of the amulet, burnt into her hand as she forced herself to throw it into the water. Apart from that, not a mark grazed her beautiful ethereal skin.

He felt his heart melt as her smile filled his soul with love for her beautiful body, mind and soul. He knew then that he would forever belong to her, perfect Beth.

Epilogue

It was dark as night. The fullness of the bright white moon shone down on the lake, the air bore a cool breeze with less than a whisper through the trees.

The silence was broken by a loud splash as the first pale hand rose out of the water to grasp the edge of the lake, followed by their tandem gasps as they pulled themselves on to the banks to lie on the cool mud, their bodies exhausted and trembling.

Still catching her breath, Beth laughed as she realised they were back at the lake near the settlement at Fahra Point. They'd made it together, the otherworld locked and the amulet destroyed.

Xanther lay on his side, mud splattering his clothes as he looked around then at Beth, smiling Beth, who looked so incredibly alive and very much a human.

"I love you."